Spelling Mistake
(The Kitchen Witch, Book 4)
Morgana Best

Spelling Mistake
(The Kitchen Witch, Book 4)
Copyright © 2016 by Morgana Best.
All Rights Reserved.
ISBN 978-1537443751

This is a work of fiction. Any resemblance to any person, living or dead, is purely coincidental. The personal names have been invented by the author, and any likeness to the name of any person, living or dead, is purely coincidental.
This book may contain references to specific commercial products, process or service by trade name, trademark, manufacturer, or otherwise, specific brand-name products and/or trade names of products, which are trademarks or registered trademarks and/or trade names, and these are property of their respective owners. Morgana Best or her associates, have no association with any specific commercial products, process, or service by trade name, trademark, manufacturer, or otherwise, specific brand-name products and / or trade names of products.

By this act
And words of rhyme
Trouble not
These books of mine
With these words I now thee render
Candle burn and bad return
3 Thymes stronger to its sender.
(Ancient Celtic)

Chapter 1

I was looking forward to my morning off work. It was the first one I'd had in ages. I threw my car keys down on the couch and sat next to them, and then placed my mail on my lap. If only I hadn't had to drive to town to fetch it, but the pesky mail lady, Kayleen, had made a Post Office Box a necessity.

The first bill was an overdue electricity notice along with a sizeable late fee. What? I hadn't even gotten the first bill yet. I scowled and looked at the second letter. I tore it open. Another bill, this time a gas bill. I didn't even have the gas connected! I shook my head. As I reached for the third letter, the sound of a battle cry forced me to my feet. "Can you please turn down that down?" I yelled at the house.

The house always decided what it wanted to watch on TV. I had inherited my magnificent Victorian house, along with a cupcake store, from my Aunt Angelica. No-one had told me the house was alive. I'd found out the hard way.

The house used to enjoy watching mixed martial arts or Jamie Oliver; now it was *Game of Thrones*. It was like sharing a house with a demanding housemate. The house turned down the volume just as I looked up at the screen to see a rather gory scene. I shuddered and turned my attention to the third letter. My spirits lifted when I saw it was from the Lotteries Office. Maybe I'd won something! The first words were not encouraging: *Call Gambling Help.* I read down the page. No, I hadn't won a thing.

So much for my relaxing morning off. My eyes fell on the bare rooted rose in the corner of the room. My neighbor, Camino, had given it to me as a gift the previous day. I sighed and picked up the plant. I knew I would have to plant it sooner or later, so I might as well get it over with. I headed outside to the little garden shed behind the house to fetch a shovel.

I wasn't one for gardening. Luckily for me, the garden was mature, with beautiful lilac trees and a native mango tree all well established, and the rest of the garden could take care of itself. All I did was water it regularly, but I wasn't one to plant new flowers.

Once in the garden, my mood soon improved. How could it not, as the air was permeated with the scent of many fragrant old English roses. Now where to put it? I didn't even know what type of rose it was, because it didn't have a label. It only had the words, 'Bare Rooted Rose,' scrawled on the plastic wrapping. I was glad there had been unseasonal heavy rain lately. I didn't much fancy digging in ground that was usually like concrete. After a quick appraisal of the area, my eyes fell on a patch of ground next to the daisies. That looked as good a place as any. I shrugged and headed for the spot.

As I suspected, the ground was soft, so the digging was easy. It was an awfully big bare rooted rose, and I figured I should make the hole deeper than the root ball. That was something I remembered from watching a gardening show the house had once made me watch.

Just one more shovelful, I thought, and made a special effort to dig. As I pushed the shovel in strongly, the soft ground suddenly made way to something hard, and the impact reverberated through my back. I dropped the shovel in shock as a sharp pain seared through me.

I assumed it was a hard rock, so I gingerly dug around it. After all, even I knew that a rose shouldn't be planted over a big rock. To my surprise, it was not a rock, but a metal box. I kneeled down, ignoring the pain in my back, and managed to pull the box from the dirt. It was covered with particularly sticky, slushy mud. I quickly shoved the rose into the hole after backfilling some dirt, filled in the hole and then patted down the dirt, and all the while my back pain was increasing.

The metal box looked old. The latch that fastened it had rusted away but was still working. I was intrigued. Perhaps my Aunt Angelica herself had buried this in my garden. Maybe it was full of expensive jewelry. My hands shook with excitement. I could keep the nicest pieces and sell one or two to pay the bills. I wondered if there were garnets in there, or perhaps rubies? I was partial to emeralds, too. Maybe there were huge pink diamonds. The tin was certainly heavy enough.

I picked up the box, leaving the shovel next to the rose, and hurried to the house. I left the box at the front door and went inside to find an old rag to clean it.

When I went back outside, the box wasn't at the door. It took me a moment to see that it was on my front lawn. "Why don't you want the box inside the house?" I asked the house, but as usual, there was no reply. Perhaps the house didn't share Aunt Angelica's taste in jewelry.

I hurried down the steps and wiped the box as best I could, and then washed my hands under the garden hose.

When the box was suitably clean, I took it inside and placed it on top of some newspaper on my coffee table. The pain in my back was much worse. In fact, my back was cramping up. It was all I could do to straighten up, and bending over drawers looking for a screwdriver didn't help. By the time I found a screwdriver to bust open the latch, I was in considerable pain.

I carefully perched on the edge of my couch, and gingerly inserted the screw under the corroded latch. After all, if there was jewelry inside, or perhaps solid gold bars, I didn't want to damage the contents. It could even be cash. What if Aunt Angelica hadn't trusted banks and had put all her savings in the tin?

I was quivering with excitement and suspense. After moving the screwdriver backward and forward for a while, I managed to release the latch. Finally! I took a deep, calming breath and prepared myself to see my newfound treasure. I opened the box and gasped.

No jewelry. No diamonds. No gold bars. No cash. There, inside the box, was a beautifully bound volume of ebony leather, with a pentacle embossed in gold on the cover. Wonderment at once replaced my initial dismay at the lack of jewelry.

I opened the book, cautiously handling the frail, ancient pages that threatened to snap at my touch. On the first page in flowery script were the words, *Book of Shadows*. This spellbook must have belonged to one of my ancestors! I trembled with anticipation as I lifted the book onto my knees and opened it. The pages were tanned and the gold leaf so long ago applied to the edges of the pages was crumbling away.

As I gingerly turned the crinkled pages, I fancied I could smell the scent of ancient white sage. It was a fragrance I usually associated with the mysterious Alder Vervain. The book fairly pulsed with energy.

I made to stand up, but a searing pain hit me at the base of my spine. This pain wasn't going to go away by itself. I carefully set the book aside and scrolled through my phone to google a physical therapist, and called the first one I saw.

"Harden Physical Therapy, please hold," a disembodied voice said.

I hadn't yet had a chance to speak, but the phone played some particularly unpleasant music. I opened the book to a random page near the beginning. "This looks like ancient writing," I said to myself. I was in the habit of speaking to myself aloud. After all, I lived alone unless you counted my two cats, Willow and Hawthorn. The cats didn't look alike, but had identical personalities. Willow, a large ginger, was three times the size of Hawthorn, a slender black cat. They were both staring at me now, and I could've sworn that there was concern in their eyes.

I was careful with the book's pages, given that they were brittle, like old parchment. "This looks like Latin or something," I said to the cats. "Oh look! Here's a spell to improve one's baking. How strange—that heading's in English, but there's a whole section below it that looks like Latin. Do you think it could improve *my* baking?"

Both cats looked doubtful. Undaunted, I proceeded to read the Latin aloud as best I could, while the music on the phone changed to another old song.

Both cats hissed, turned, and sprinted for the door. I tried to stand up, but my eyes watered from the pain. "Here's something in English," I said to their departing cat bottoms. "'Beware the *vox nihili*,' whatever that means. Someone else must've written that, as it's in different handwriting right below that Latin section."

The music stopped, and a woman's voice spoke. "Hello, Helen Harden speaking. How may I help you?"

I did not answer, because a hideous entity manifested before my very eyes.

Chapter 2

The apparition hovered in front of me. I was filled with terror. I assumed it was a demon, not that I'd ever seen a demon in real life, only in movies, but it looked like one to me. It was a humanoid type of thing, only much scarier than a human. It had a big round face, a mouth filled with sharp jagged teeth, and a small amount of spiky hair that stuck out in all directions. Its body was bloated and its legs and arms were spindly.

It smiled at me, but I didn't know whether that made me relieved or more frightened.

I finally found my voice. "What are you?" I squeaked.

The creature bowed low. "Great Dark Witch," it addressed me. Its voice was deep. "You summoned me."

I took a step backward and shook my head. "No, I didn't!"

The apparition jabbed its finger at me. "You summoned me as your assistant. *Supernatural* assistant." It shot me a glance that was likely malevolent.

"A baking assistant?" I said in disbelief. I fervently hoped that the spell I'd read aloud for improving one's baking didn't work by means of summoning an apparition as an assistant.

"If you wish."

It was then I realized someone was still on the other end of the phone. "Hello? Hello?" the voice said loudly.

"Hello, sorry about that," I said.

"How can I help you?"

"I just hurt my back badly while digging in the garden," I managed to say, while keeping an eye on the creature. "I was calling to make an appointment. I'm in a lot of pain." I turned slightly and then punctuated that with a heartfelt "Ouch!"

"If you leave right now, I can fit you in. Are you in town? I only have a small opening due to a last minute cancelation," the voice continued after a pause.

I was about to refuse and book an appointment for the following day, given the apparition hovering in front of me, when my back spasmed painfully. I shot one more look at the being, and then decided. "Yes, I'm in town. I can be there in five minutes."

I hung up, and then realized that I had no time to put on nice clothes or make-up. I shook my head. Why was I even thinking about clothes or make-up when there was a supernatural being in front of me? I must be losing my mind.

Still, there was no time to worry about the spirit now. I just hoped no one else could see it. My back spasmed once more, so I grabbed my purse and headed out the door.

Halfway to my car, I shot a glance over my shoulder—which by the way, hurt quite a bit—and there was no sign of the demon. I let out a long sigh of relief, but that only served to hurt my back even more.

The driving made my back worse, even though it was only a short distance. When I got out of the car, I had difficulty straightening up. I hobbled into the front door of Harden Physical Therapy. I saw at once that it was a small business, with a tiny desk, computer, and chair in the corner, and a doorway labeled 'Treatment Room' at the back of the room.

A woman hurried through the door. She had a mess of curly auburn hair and particularly good skin. I had no chance of guessing her age—she looked anything from thirty to fifty. "Amelia Spelled?"

"Yes, that's me."

She ushered me into the treatment room and gestured to a chair. She then proceeded to ask me questions, but I was distracted, wondering if the apparition would suddenly appear, and what I would do if it did. I really needed to call Ruprecht and get his advice on the situation, but I was in too much pain to think clearly. I looked up to realize that Helen was staring at me, her pen in hand. "Sorry?"

"I just asked if you had lost any unexplained weight lately."

I shook my head. "I wish!"

Helen was not amused. She made me lie down on her treatment table and massaged my back for a bit. "You've pulled muscles around the bottom two vertebrae. When your back gets better, you'll have to walk and do exercises to strengthen your core, and do Tai Chi or Pilates. What do you do for work? Standing or sitting in the one position for too long isn't good."

"I have the cupcake store," I began, but she cut me off.

"Oh yes, my husband mentioned it recently. He's a Systems Analyst Specialist at the Council. Now I'm going to put the TENS machine on you while I ask you more questions about your injury."

The questions mercifully came to an end, although I did like the sensation of the ripples from the TENS machine. Helen held an ultrasound machine across my back after that, and then stuck on a heat pad that adhered to my clothing. "I'm going to give you traction now," she said.

For a moment, I was worried that the demon had possessed her. "Traction?" I said, horrified.

Helen frowned. "Don't worry, the rack was used as a torture device centuries ago, but these days we use it to take pressure off your spine. It will help with the pinched nerve. I'm just going to buckle you up, and then attach this device to your legs. You'll feel relief pretty quickly."

I sure hoped she was telling the truth. Helen continued to talk as she strapped me in. "How's your business going?"

"Since the Council moved to the new building right near me, all the staff are coming in, so we're doing a roaring trade."

Helen simply nodded and left the room, after telling me she would be back in fifteen minutes.

I had to admit, the traction did appear to be working. After a few moments, the awful crunching sensation in my lower back started to ease, and I relaxed into the sensation. What a terrible start to the day I'd had! I had hurt my back badly, and I had summoned an entity.

A touch on my ankle wrenched me from my daydreams. I opened my eyes, expecting to see Helen. Instead, it was a man.

"Let's get these terrible things off you," he said firmly.

He undid all my straps, and I sat up, confused. "But Helen said I needed traction?" I asked. I hardly thought it likely that Helen would employ a physical therapist who did not share her views on treatment.

The man bent over me. "I've saved your life! She was trying to torture you. I've fulfilled my duty by helping you."

I stared at him. Was this some kind of joke?

"It's me, Great One, your assistant," the man said. "I thought you'd prefer this human form."

Realization dawned on me slowly. "You're the demon!"

The man was visibly offended. "How could you say such a thing, Great Dark Witch?" He clutched his chest. "I've never been so insulted or hurt in all my lives! I'm not a demon, I'm your assistant."

Just then, Helen hurried into the room. "I thought I could hear voices," she said, staring at the man. "How did you get in here?"

He pushed past her and hurried out the door. I was grateful that he had kept his human form, and thankful he was wearing clothes.

Helen turned to me. "Do you know him?"

I shook my head. "I've never seen him before," I said. *Not in that appearance, at least*, I silently added.

Helen shook her head, and strapped me back into traction. She started the traction machine, then hurried to the window and slammed it shut. "Perhaps he got in through here," she said. "I apologize I left you alone for so long. I just had a call from the security man. That husband of mine! He didn't replace the batteries when I said we should, and now we have no batteries at all. The security man said they're all corroded and he has to order them from Melbourne. It'll take weeks!" She sighed deeply.

She kept making small talk throughout my treatment, but I barely listened to her. I was worried about the entity. I now knew that it could take human form. Was it a shapeshifter? I shuddered.

And what was it going to do next?

Chapter 3

I sat in my car, despite Helen's stern warning not to sit it any longer than necessary, and called Ruprecht. To my dismay, it went to voicemail. I left a message to call me back, and briefly told him that I had summoned an entity. I then drove to my cupcake store as fast as I could. Thyme would know what to do.

I got out of the car and stood up. I was expecting my back to spasm, but it definitely had improved. The adhesive heat pack stuck onto my lower back was bringing relief, although the pungent smell of herbs wasn't entirely pleasant.

I hadn't seen the entity since his appearance in the treatment room, but I knew that he would do something else. Hopefully, Thyme and the others would have experience in this type of thing and would able to despatch him.

There was a customer in the shop, so I wasn't able to tell Thyme what had happened. Thyme took the customer's money, and then turned to me. "Hey boss, you're late!"

"Something happened," I said, wiggling my eyebrows and fixing her with a look in the hope she'd catch onto the fact that it was a supernatural something. "And I hurt my back and had to go to the physical therapist. And before that, something important happened…"

Thyme interrupted me. "I'm running late for an appointment, so can you wrap these cupcakes for the customer?" She shot the customer a winning smile and then made to walk away.

"But Thyme, something's happened."

"You can tell me all about it when I get back." With that, she took her purse and hurried out the door.

I shrugged, but there was nothing I could do. The entity would have to wait. I only hoped that it didn't do something horrid before the others could send it back to where it came from.

As soon as the customer left, I tried to call Ruprecht again, but once more it went to voicemail. I was about to call Camino and Mint and ask them to go over to *Glinda's*, Ruprecht's store, to tell him in person, but all at once three customers came into the shop.

To my dismay, two of them were Craig and the obnoxious Kayleen. I had dated Craig briefly before I found out that he was also dating the mail lady, Kayleen, and goodness knows who else. He had turned out to be quite a jerk.

Kayleen and I had never liked each other. She was an awful snoop. In fact, I had caught her reading my mail on more than one occasion. She had taken even more of a dislike to me when she found out that Craig and I had dated.

Craig politely ordered a dozen cherry coconut cupcakes, while Kayleen stood behind him and scowled at me. "Have your cakes poisoned anyone lately, Amelia?" she said with a nasal chuckle.

I forced a fake laugh, annoyed that she said it while another customer was standing right behind them. I recognized him as Scott Plank, the Town Planner. He was a particularly unpleasant man who was full of his own self-importance, and had become a regular customer after the Council Chambers had moved to a building just down the road from my store.

Scott cleared his throat and shuffled, obviously indicating that I should serve him before Craig and Kayleen, even though they had been there first. Today, his face was bright red and he was scowling. "Can I sample that lemon cheesecake mini cupcake!" he said, in a tone that was more of a demand than a request.

I took Craig's money, and then handed Scott the closest lemon cheesecake mini cupcake. Scott proceeded to answer his phone, and then yelled loudly at the unfortunate person on the other end of it.

I had just finished wrapping Craig's order, when Scott spat out the cupcake. "It's stale!" he yelled at me. He threw the rest of the cake on the floor in a tantrum.

Craig clutched his box of cupcakes to his chest as his jaw dropped open. Even Kayleen appeared to be shocked. I'd had bad customers before, but never anything on this scale. "I'll get something to clean up that mess," I said in the most even tone I could muster.

I hurried to the kitchen, hoping that Scott would be gone when I got back. This surely would have to be the worst day on record. Perhaps I should've stayed in bed. On the plus side, the entity hadn't reappeared, not yet anyway.

It took me a while to find the dustpan and brush set as it wasn't in its usual place. I walked back into the store, and could see no heads above the display case. Luckily, the unpleasant Town Planner had left.

When I rounded the corner of the display case, I gasped. All the blood ran from my face, and I clutched the display cabinet. There, lying on the floor, was Scott Plank. He was dead, and there was a length of rope around his neck.

I stood frozen to the spot in horror. Had the entity done this? Had the entity thought he was helping me by killing a rude customer?

I had summoned the entity. Was I responsible for a man's murder?

Chapter 4

I ran to the street and looked out, but I couldn't see anyone fleeing the scene. I flipped the sign to 'Closed' and at the same time pulled my phone out of my pocket to call the police.

Had the entity done it? Or had Craig and Kayleen? I had left them in the shop with the man. A woman's voice forced me to turn my attention back to the phone. "What makes you think the man was murdered?"

"There's a rope wrapped tightly around his neck," I said.

The voice told me to wait there until the police came. I mean, it wasn't as if I was going to leave, but I suppose they have to say that to everyone.

Thyme returned and knocked on the door just as I hung up. As I opened the door, Thyme spoke before I could say anything. "Why is the shop shut?" She looked past me and saw the man lying on the floor. "Oh, not again!"

"Yes, again," I said sadly. "And what's more, I think I killed him."

Thyme gasped again. "Oh no, you didn't do any baking, did you?"

I didn't know whether or not to be offended. "No, of course not! I have to speak in a hurry before the police get here. I wanted to tell you what happened this morning, but then you left. This is the potted summary. I was gardening and I dug up a tin, and there was a Book of Shadows inside it."

"A Book of Shadows?" Thyme asked incredulously.

I held up my hand to forestall any more questions. "Quite a lot's happened, so I have to tell you quickly, because the police will be here any minute. Don't ask any more questions until I finish." Thyme nodded as I pushed on, but it was obvious she wanted to ask more. "Long story short, I hurt my back while I was digging out the tin box, and so while I was calling the physical therapist, I read out a Latin spell and it turned out that I summoned an entity."

"What sort of entity?" Thyme asked, and then slapped her hand over her mouth.

"How should I know?" I said, exasperated. "It looked pretty weird, but then when I was at the physical therapist, she had me on one of those therapy machines, and the entity appeared. This time, he looked like a human, a man, and he tried to get me out of the therapy machine. He said he was my assistant."

Thyme interrupted me once more. "What do you mean, he looked like a man?"

"That's just it," I said. "He looked like a normal human being at that point. I tried to call Ruprecht twice, but it went to voicemail. I'm really panicking, Thyme! What if that supernatural assistant entity thing thought he was helping me by killing Scott Plank?"

Thyme looked confused. "Why would it think killing someone would help you?"

I rubbed my forehead. It was all so surreal. I was having a conversation about a supernatural entity that I had accidentally summoned, while standing next to the body of a murder victim. "Scott Plank came in here in a foul mood, and demanded a sample of a cupcake, and then threw it on the floor. I went into the kitchen to get something to clean it up, and when I came back I found him there. I'm just scared that the entity strangled him because he was rude to me, or something." When I said it, it did sound lame, and that gave me a little bit of hope.

Thyme frowned. She patted my shoulder quickly. "I'm sure this thing didn't do it, Amelia. Don't worry." Her tone was less than convincing.

I remembered something important. "Oh, and when I left to get something to clean up the mess, Kayleen and Craig were still in the shop."

Thyme opened her mouth to speak, but the arrival of the police forestalled her. I recognized Sergeant Tinsdell, but the constable was new, and he had a far more pleasant face than Constable Walker's. I had heard that Walker had been transferred, but I hadn't heard anything about his replacement.

Tinsdell sighed heavily when he saw me. "This is getting to be quite a habit, Miss Spelled." He looked at us both and then nodded at the other officer. "This is Constable Dawson."

"Well, hello," Thyme said, looking the constable up and down. "The sticky buns aren't the only sweet thing in your shop," she whispered to me.

I elbowed her in the rib. I could only assume that the stress was getting to her.

"We're here to investigate," the constable announced.

"You're not here for a croissant, then?" I said sarcastically.

The constable appeared not to take offense. "You're not trying to bribe a police officer, are you, ladies?" He beamed at Thyme, who giggled.

Sergeant Tinsdell glared at the constable. "Dawson, a murder has just occurred."

Dawson looked shamefaced for a moment, before shooting another smile at Thyme when the sergeant wasn't looking. I had never seen Thyme interested in anyone before, and she sure seemed taken with this police officer. It appeared to be mutual.

"The detectives are on their way," Sergeant Tinsdell said, "so I suggest we go into a back room and await their arrival. I'll take your statements. I assume neither of you touched anything?"

Thyme and I shook our heads. "Thyme wasn't even here when it happened," I said. "She arrived back here after I called you."

The police officers followed me into the little office. I hastily wiped the small table while Thyme snuffed the lemongrass candle burning in one corner.

The sergeant pulled out a notepad and a pen. "You know the routine by now, Miss Spelled. Tell me what happened, right from the beginning, and then you can give your statement to the detectives later. We won't need to take your fingerprints to exclude them from the crime scene, as we already have them on record." He shot me a pointed look as he said it.

I recounted the events, how I had gone to the physical therapist, and then returned to the shop, replaced Thyme, and then served Craig and Kayleen as well as Scott Plank. I told them how Scott had yelled at someone on the phone and then thrown his cupcake to the floor. I told him that Craig and Kayleen and Scott had all been in the room together when I left to get something to clean up the cupcake remains on the floor, and when I returned, Scott was dead.

"Right," Tinsdell said. "The forensics team will bag that cupcake out there, and we'll need to bag all the cupcakes from that batch. The shop will have to be shut until we get the test results back."

"But he wasn't poisoned," I protested. "He was strangled."

"Just because there was a rope around his neck doesn't mean that he was strangled," Tinsdell said in a superior tone. "We can't make assumptions in this line of work."

I was seething. It was obvious that Scott had been strangled, given the angry red mark around his neck, not to mention the rope. Still, I had to tell myself that the police were only doing their duty. I suppose they did have to test the cakes, but Tinsdell's attitude left a lot to be desired.

"How long before I'm allowed back in my store?" I asked him. "I have the opening of the Council building coming up, and I have to cater the cakes."

"It will take as long as it takes," Tinsdell said evenly. "You should know the ropes by now."

"So, I haven't seen you around before. Have you just moved to town?" Thyme addressed the question to Constable Dawson.

He seemed pleased to be asked. "Yes, Constable Walker was transferred to Byron Bay, and I was transferred here."

I raised my eyebrows. Next she'd ask him if he had a girlfriend. While I was pleased that Thyme had at last found a love interest, I didn't think this was the time or place. After all, it was a solemn occasion. Not only had a man been murdered, in my own store at that, but there was a possibly homicidal entity on the loose.

I was wracked with guilt. If I hadn't summoned the spirit, would the man still be alive?

Chapter 5

The detectives had whisked me straight off to the police station for questioning. Thyme had managed to tell me that the detectives had coincidentally been in the area. She had that information courtesy of Constable Dawson. Still, there was no time to dwell on the possible romantic interests of my best friend, Thyme. At least she was going to be questioned after I was, so she should be able to get in a call to Camino or Mint and ask them to go over to *Glinda's* to tell Ruprecht what had happened.

I looked at the detectives once more. They had introduced themselves as Greene and Jones, and they were hard to tell apart. Both appeared to be around fifty, were very tanned, and both had sandy colored hair. They looked more like surfers than detectives, but their attitude was certainly not laid back. I wondered if either of them had ever cracked a smile. In fact, they both looked devoid of any emotion whatsoever. "Would you mind telling me where you have been for the last three hours," Detective Greene said.

I told him everything in as much detail as I could, a little nervous that a video camera was trained on me. Detective Jones scribbled away furiously the whole time I was speaking.

"Can you tell me anything about his manner?"

I scratched my chin. "He was very angry. I don't know him well. He's only been a regular customer since the Council moved close to my shop, and while I'd never exactly call him friendly, he's never been rude before, not until today."

"Was he dressed as usual?" Greene asked.

I thought that a strange question. "I suppose so. I mean, as I said, I don't really know him all that well. He was wearing a suit. I didn't notice anything strange about it." I winced. My back was hurting from sitting in the hard chair. I had left the adhesive heat pack at the shop, and now was regretting that decision.

"You do realize your shop will have to remain shut until we have the results on the samples we've taken," Greene said sternly.

I nodded. I wasn't happy about it, but I knew that they were doing their job, as frustrating as it was.

"This must all be routine to you by now, Miss Spelled," Greene said.

I shot him a look, but he didn't elaborate further. Just then, a uniformed officer entered the room. He was carrying a cardboard tray with three take-out cups of coffee. He placed one in front of me, and then one in front of each detective. To my surprise, he then produced a heat pack which he duly handed to me. He turned to the detectives. "Sergeant's orders. Miss Spelled has a back injury." With that, he winked at me and left the room.

The detectives exchanged glances. "Who was that?" Jones asked Greene in an undertone. "I haven't seen him before."

Greene shrugged and then sipped his coffee. I sipped mine. It was a latté, made just how I like it. A chill ran up my spine. Was the officer the entity?

Detective Greene was still speaking. "Do you know anyone who would have reason to harm Mr. Plank?"

I set down my coffee and shook my head. "As I keep saying, I don't really know him. I've already said that he's only just become a fairly regular customer. I know he's the Town Planner, and I've never heard anyone with a good word to say about him, but I've never heard anyone say they wished him harm or anything like that."

Greene sipped his coffee before speaking. "What about your fireman friend and his partner?"

"Craig's no friend of mine, nor is Kayleen. Are you asking if they had something against Scott Plank?"

"Yes," Greene said.

"I have no idea," I said. "I don't speak to those two. Craig occasionally comes in to buy cupcakes for the other firemen." I shivered. It was cool in the room, just cold enough to be uncomfortable. I wrapped my hands around the coffee.

"Can you tell me exactly what happened immediately prior to the time that you left the room? Think carefully, Miss Spelled."

I remembered it only too well. "While I was wrapping Craig's order, Scott demanded a cupcake sample. I gave him one, and he took a bite and then threw it on the floor. I hurried to the kitchen to get something to clean it up."

Greene looked down at his notes. "And when you left, where were Craig and Kayleen?"

"Well, they were still in the shop," I said.

Detective Greene narrowed his eyes. "Whereabouts in your shop were they? Were they walking to the door? Were they standing still?"

I rubbed my eyes. The heat pack was helping my back, but the pain was nevertheless increasing due to sitting on the hard chair. "They were still standing at the counter. They looked shocked at Scott Plank's tantrum. When I got back from the kitchen, there was no sign of them. I actually ran out my front door to see if I could see anyone fleeing the scene, but I couldn't see anyone at all."

"Thank you, Miss Spelled. We'll leave it there for the time being. We'll be in touch."

I stood up, and grabbed my back as it cramped. I made sure I took my latté with me, and went to the waiting room. There was no sign of Thyme, but I assumed they had her in another room.

It was only around fifteen minutes or so before Thyme appeared. She hurried over to me. "Ruprecht called me. He was watching a movie and he'd turned off his phone. Mint went around there and told him everything that happened. He wants us to go straight around there now, but he wants you to bring the Book of Shadows." Thyme paused to draw breath. "Are you all right, Amelia? Were they rough on you with the questioning?"

I shifted from one foot to the other to ease the pain in my back. "No, they were pretty good. How about you?"

"They were okay. When they let me go, I saw Sergeant Tinsdell take Craig in for questioning."

I walked outside with Thyme. "Do you think Kayleen and Craig did it?"

Thyme paused for a moment. "It's possible, I suppose. No one liked Scott Plank. It was rumored he did shady deals. I don't know what motive they could've had, though. Are you still worried that the entity you summoned did it?"

I nodded. "Yes, and that reminds me. Some police officer I've never seen before came in and brought the three of us take out coffees and a heat pack for my back."

Thyme looked surprised. "He did? That's weird! How did anyone know about your back? And they've always given me horrible black coffee that tastes like it was made a week earlier."

"Did any officer give you coffee today?"

"No. Amelia, that's so weird!"

We had reached Thyme's car. Surely Ruprecht would know what to do. And I hadn't even told Alder Vervain what was happening. I didn't want to call him in front of Thyme, given her attitude toward him. None of my friends liked Alder, because he came from a long line of witch hunters. They remained suspicious of him, despite my reassurances that he did not share the family views. Of course, I hadn't told them that he himself was a Dark Witch—Alder had asked me to keep that confidential.

Alder and I had become friends, but I hoped we'd become more. I'd had dinner with him a couple of times, but we'd always been interrupted by more pressing matters—murder, to be precise. To say I had a crush on him was the understatement of the century. Even thinking about him made my heart flutter wildly.

I sent Alder a long text explaining as briefly as I could about the morning's events, and telling him that Thyme was driving me straight to Ruprecht's. Alder would then know not to call.

Thyme looked over at me. "Who are you texting?"

"Alder," I said somewhat defensively.

Thyme pursed her lips. "He reminds me of a cross between Angel, and Spike on a good day."

I frowned. "What on earth are you talking about?"

"You know, Spike was much cuter in the last season of *Buffy*."

I sighed. This had to be one of the worst days I'd ever had, and that was saying something.

Chapter 6

Ruprecht was standing in the door of *Glinda's*. Even as Thyme drew her car to a stop, I could see that Ruprecht's face was white and drawn.

"Oh my dear!" Ruprecht greeted me. "I'm so sorry. I was watching such an uplifting film, *Mitt liv som hund*, or in English, *My Life as a Dog*. It is an inspiring 1985 Swedish film where a boy loses everything, his mother, his elderly friend, his beloved dog, but then thinks of worse things that have happened—such as the Russians sending that dog, Laika, into space to a certain death, and a track athlete who was accidentally speared by a javelin—and considers that his life isn't so bad after all. We could all learn something from that."

I nodded, figuring that his words were somehow intended to give me comfort, goodness knows how. They were more likely to give me nightmares or expensive therapy bills.

"I had my phone turned off so I could hear the movie," he continued.

I was impressed. "I didn't know you could speak Swedish, Ruprecht."

He laughed. "Of course I can't, Amelia. It had subtitles."

Now I was even more confused. I shrugged and followed Ruprecht into his store, a strange combination of antiques and old books. It always reminded me of the set of a Harry Potter movie. The faint scent of white sage hung in the air, and it held none of the somewhat depressing and entirely claustrophobic atmosphere of many antique stores. The only sound was a faint rendition of lyres and double clarinets, Ruprecht's favorite music, a reconstruction of ancient Greek music, or so he had informed me many a time.

Ruprecht's apartment was directly behind his store, and we'd had countless important meetings there. Today would likely be the most important.

I passed the collection of weird and wonderful astronomical instruments and walked into the kitchen, where Camino and Mint were already sitting at the round table, their faces white and drawn.

There was a pungent smell in the room, sweet but strong. I looked at the thin ribbons of smoke rising from incense burning on charcoal tablets within little cauldrons placed about the room. Camino followed my gaze. "Fiery Wall of Protection," she said. "Dragons Blood, frankincense, and myrrh."

I took my seat at the table, and then quickly went through the morning's events once more that day. When I concluded, Ruprecht wordlessly arose from the table and walked over to the countertop. He returned with a cup of brew which he placed in front of me. "What's that?" I asked him as I watched the steam rise from it in spirals. "A potion to keep me safe from the supernatural assistant?"

Ruprecht shook his head. "It's a cup of hot English Breakfast tea with three heaped spoons of sugar. Drink it, it will help with the shock."

I clutched the cup and came straight to the point. "Do you think this supernatural entity assistant thing killed Scott Plank?" I hoped they would rush to assure me that it hadn't, but to my dismay, they all remained silent.

"Let's go into the living room where we can examine the Book of Shadows," Ruprecht said.

I couldn't help thinking it was a funeral procession as we filed one by one into the adjoining room. Ruprecht laid a piece of deep purple silk over the large table that sat resplendent in the center of the room. Golden sparkles flew from the silk as it swooshed through the air, and I didn't know whether they were real or due to some kind of magic. I put the tin on the floor against one table leg. As I pulled out the Book of Shadows and set it on the table, everybody gasped.

"That must be Thelma's book, the ancestral book of the Spelled family that was given to her by her husband, Wolff Spelled," Camino said to Ruprecht. Her tone was one of wonder.

"Yes, of course it is," Ruprecht said absently.

"Thelma Spelled, my great aunt?" I said. "Aunt Angelica's mother?"

Ruprecht and Camino nodded solemnly.

I was perplexed. "But why would she bury it?"

"That's the million dollar question," Ruprecht said. "Angelica told me about the Book of Shadows, but she never mentioned what had become of it." He raised one eyebrow at Camino, who nodded.

"She never mentioned it to me, either. I knew about the Spelled family's Book of Shadows of course, but I didn't know where it was."

Ruprecht carefully, almost reverently, opened the Book of Shadows. "It's in an amazing state of preservation," he said, "given that it's been buried all these years. Thelma must have enclosed it in a spell of protection." He shut the book and turned to me. "Now, Amelia, show me the spell that you read out aloud."

I felt defensive and more than a little guilty. "I really didn't mean to read the spell," I said. "I was on hold to Helen Harden, the physical therapist, and I was flipping through the book while I was waiting for her to speak again." I noted Ruprecht's abject look of horror at the fact that anyone would do something so impertinent as to flip through such a book. "I came across a spell to improve one's baking," I continued, "but it was in Latin, I think. I didn't know what it said, but I read it aloud. That's when the entity appeared." I carefully opened the book. It was a thick book, so it took me a while to find the spell. "There it is." I pointed to the heading that said, *Spell to improve one's baking*.

The others looked over my shoulder, but Ruprecht leaned so close to the book that I thought his nose would touch it. "It's in Latin," he proclaimed. "My Latin is a little rusty."

I held my breath as Ruprecht bent over the text. "Oh no!" he exclaimed after an interval.

"What is it? Is it bad?" I rubbed my hands together with anxiety.

"There." Ruprecht pointed to a line beneath the Latin. "'Beware the *vox nihili*.'"

I was puzzled. "What's a *vox nihili*?"

Ruprecht rubbed his chin. "Literally it is the voice of nothing, a typo if you will. It's a type of spelling mistake. You know when AutoCorrect on your phone makes a mess of something, turns something into meaningless writing?" We all nodded. "It's the same. When someone was copying this spell into the Book of Shadows, they copied a word wrongly, perhaps even simply copied a letter wrongly. Later, maybe even decades later, someone noticed the mistake, and made the note below it. Do you realize what this means, Amelia?"

"No," I said truthfully. I was still stuck on the fact that ancient people made typos.

I had never seen Ruprecht look so worried. "It means that you didn't summon an assistant to help you become a better baker."

I hardly dared ask the question. "Then, um, then what exactly did I summon?" I stuttered, clutching my stomach as a wave of nausea hit me.

Ruprecht shut the book and met my eyes squarely. "I don't know, and that's what worries me. To tell you the truth, Amelia, it could be anything, even an ancient demon." He held up his hand. "But then again, it could be a harmless trickster. We won't know until I read through all this Latin, and that could take me quite a while. Would you mind leaving the Book of Shadows with me?"

I readily agreed. Things weren't looking good, not at all.

Chapter 7

I adjusted my girls in the mirror at the restaurant entrance, wishing I'd worn a push up bra. Tall, dark, and handsome does not come around every day, after all. Alder ticked all three of those boxes, not to mention he was also wickedly gorgeous and paying for lunch. Actually, two push up bras would have been better. I supposed I didn't look too bad, but then again, the lighting in here was dim.

"Ahem."

I turned to see a tall waiter. He frowned and I smiled, an apology he did not seem interested in taking. He indicated that I should follow him, and I did so, glancing back to check out my derrière. He weaved his way past other patrons, past a myriad of mismatched paintings hanging on the mustard yet golden-speckled walls, and past stacks of ancient books whose musty scent rode roughshod over the pleasant aroma of Italian cooking.

I paused to look at the uncomfortable wooden chair against a table at the back of the room, and placed my purse on the red and white checked tablecloth. The waiter had already abandoned me—he had spotted Alder and was hurrying to greet him enthusiastically.

"Sorry I'm late," Alder said, hurrying over and kissing me on the cheek.

I quivered at the feel of his lips and the firm hand on the small of my back. "Alder. Nice to see you."

Alder had been out of town for a while on a case, and had returned late the previous night. "It's been a while—too long. Have you fallen impossibly in love with another man, Amelia? Am I going to have to fight for your affections?" He winked at me.

I took a deep breath. "There is no man, but yes, my affections still need to be fought for." I congratulated myself for my fast thinking—in fact, for the fact that I was able to think at all, given what Alder had just said. My knees knocked together wildly.

The waiter chose that moment to reappear. Alder glanced quickly at the menu before he ordered. "I'll have the rump steak with green peppercorn sauce and Greek salad."

The waiter looked at me with one eyebrow raised. "I'll have the chicken carbonara. It's only lunch time. I'll leave the rump steak for later."

"I'll bet," the waiter muttered.

I glared at him, and was relieved that Alder hadn't seemed to notice the remark. He smiled at me. "I was shocked when you told me everything that's happened."

"I'll show you the Book of Shadows as soon as Ruprecht's finished with it," I said. "They say it belonged to my great aunt Thelma."

"I'd love to see it." Alder smiled at me and I did my best to stop my stomach doing flip-flops. "So do you really think the entity you summoned murdered that man?"

I rested my head in my hands. "Oh gosh, don't say that! I sure hope not. I'll know more when Ruprecht manages to translate the Latin."

"I have some ancient arcane books from the family collection that you're welcome to look through," Alder said. "In fact, maybe we should go through them together. Meanwhile, I'll do a bit of snooping around about Kayleen and Craig. I've never trusted that man."

I allowed myself a small smile at the scowl on his face and hoped that it was because I had briefly dated Craig. "But would Craig or Kayleen have any motive to murder Scott Plank?" I wondered aloud. "And if they did, they'd have to have been in it together." I was going to say more, but the waiter returned.

"Your champagne, sir." The waiter shot me a speculative look before leaving.

"Champagne?"

Alder smiled. "We haven't seen each other for a while, and I wanted to celebrate."

I was touched.

"Did you know that Kayleen and Scott Plank used to date?"

My mouth fell open. "No, I had no idea! Are you sure?"

Alder nodded. "Yes, quite sure. It was years ago."

"Then it couldn't have been anything arising out of that," I said, "or she would've done away with him years ago."

"I'll do what I can to turn up information on both of them. I'll see if they had any associations with Scott through the Council, what with him being the Town Planner."

I nodded. "Good idea." Just then I saw a light in my purse. I glanced down to see a missed call on my phone. It was from Ruprecht. I didn't want to call him back in front of Alder, as I'd have to explain where I was. I didn't want to keep Alder a secret from Ruprecht, but given the fact that Ruprecht and my friends were all suspicious of him, it would bring extra stress that I didn't need right now.

I excused myself, picked up my purse, and went to the bathroom. To my horror, in the fluorescent light I could see that my eyes had dark circles under them and my face was white and drawn. I called Ruprecht and applied some more make-up while I was waiting for him to answer. Perhaps he was watching another allegedly uplifting film, or doing something just as fun such as reading the original text of Aristotle's *Metaphysics* in ancient Greek.

I was about to hang up when he answered. "Amelia! I've translated the text. I know what you've summoned."

"What?" I shrieked, just as a woman entered the bathroom and fixed me with a withering look.

"I'll explain the Latin in detail later, but it appears to be a word that indicates you've summoned an entity and given it rather a large measure of free will at the same time." Ruprecht went on to explain similarities between Latin words, and how a scribe could have made a mistake while copying it, while I tried to gather my patience.

"But have I summoned an evil entity?" I asked him when he stopped to draw breath.

There was silence for a moment, and I pictured Ruprecht shaking his head. Finally he spoke. "I don't think so. Put it this way, I have no idea, but it isn't *specifically* evil."

"Does that mean it didn't kill Scott Plank?" I asked expectantly.

Ruprecht dashed my hopes. "I'm afraid to say, Amelia, that it means nothing of the sort. We need to find out more about this entity. I assume you haven't seen it since it appeared at the police station?"

"No, I haven't. Do you think he's gone back to where he came from?"

Again, there was a moment before Ruprecht spoke. "No, I don't think so. We'll need to find a way to send him back. I'm sure he won't go until we do something to make him go. I think we need to treat this as a priority, in case he *did* have something to do with the unfortunate man's murder. Amelia, you can come over now and collect the Book of Shadows if you like, or would you prefer to leave it with me so I can study it further?"

"I'd rather leave it with you, Ruprecht," I said. "As far as I could see, most of those spells were in Latin or some other strange language. I certainly wouldn't have a hope of understanding them. I just wish there was something I could do."

"We'll just have to assume that there was human involvement in that man's demise," Ruprecht said. "But meanwhile, we need to investigate further. I think we might have been distracted by the entity. We can't forget the fact that a man was murdered in your store, and I hope someone wasn't trying to set you up to take the blame."

I leaned against the countertop. That hadn't occurred to me. Before I could say as much, Ruprecht pressed on. "I don't want to alarm you at all, but why would anyone choose to murder somebody in your store? Now, I know it's happened before, but the police are fully aware you had nothing to do with that, and that murderer is currently in prison. It just doesn't make sense to me. If I can turn my attention to the Book of Shadows, perhaps you, Camino, Thyme, and my granddaughter, Mint, can look into the matter of Scott Plank's death. From a distance, I mean," he added sternly. "Research on the internet, that type of thing."

I agreed and then hurried back to my table.

"We still haven't had dinner, Amelia," Alder said as soon as I sat down.

I clutched my knees to stop them knocking together under the table. "No," I simply said.

Alder frowned. "Would you like to have dinner at my place tomorrow night? I'll cook, and then after dinner we can look through my family's collection of old books. Perhaps we can turn up something on the entity there."

I managed to murmur my agreement. Alder was devilishly handsome, dark, and mysterious. Was he seriously interested in me, Amelia Spelled? It all seemed too good to be true.

One thing I knew, he didn't want me for my cooking.

Chapter 8

I was walking from the restaurant back to my shop, to see if the police would allow me back in yet. I was sure that they wouldn't, but it was worth a try. I was full of the warm and fuzzies after having lunch with Alder.

I saw Craig ahead of me and hurried to catch him. He saw me too, and suddenly turned and tried to cross the road. Unluckily for him, a truck went past at that moment and he had to wait. I quickened my pace and called to him.

"Hello, Amelia. I didn't see you there," he said in what was an obvious lie.

"That must've been a terrible thing for you to see," I said. It was the first thing that came into my mind as a lead in to the subject of Scott Plank.

"What do you mean?" Craig said all too defensively. "I didn't see him being murdered, of course. I wasn't in your store when it happened. Did you tell the police that I was?" His tone had changed to belligerent.

"Of course not," I said, trying to keep my tone even. "I assume you left the shop before whoever it was strangled him."

Craig nodded furiously. "That's right."

"Did you see anyone go to the store?"

"No." Craig clearly wanted to be anywhere other than speaking to me.

"Still, it must've been a shock for you. I assume you knew the man." I did my best to make my tone sympathetic.

"No, I didn't know him at all. Not at all." And with that, Craig hurried across cross the road, shooting a backward glance at me.

I would have to check into that. Craig was none too comfortable talking about the victim, and I found it hard to believe that two long term residents in the same small town didn't know each other. Craig didn't like me, and Kayleen particularly despised me, so if they did have reason to kill the man, then I had no doubt that they would plan to do so in my shop.

Yet they were in my shop buying cupcakes before the victim even came in. That surely meant that they hadn't planned to kill him at that moment. Perhaps they took advantage of the opportunity, but that would mean that Craig had rope in his pocket. It just didn't add up. There had to be more to it.

I reached my shop and saw to my dismay that yellow tape was still across my doorway. There were two police vehicles parked outside. I shouldn't have been surprised, because the detectives had said they would call me when they had finished with the scene of the crime, as they put it. I was about to turn away and head for home when I saw Thyme waving from across the street. She hurried over to me. "Have you seen that spirit creature thingy again?"

I laughed. "Is that a technical term?" She laughed, too. "You'll be glad to know I haven't seen it since the police questioning," I said. "I hope that isn't just a temporary absence and that it's gone for good."

Thyme shook her head. "Don't get your hopes up on that one, Amelia. Ruprecht said it won't go away by itself—someone will need to send it away with a spell. At least there haven't been any more murders in town."

"Great," I said, considering that was a good thing. Of course, murder is never a good thing, but I thought that if the entity was, in fact, homicidal, then it would have gone on a killing spree by now. "Well, it looks as if the two of us have the rest of the day off and probably tomorrow as well," I added, "and goodness knows how long after that."

Thyme nodded to the police tape. "It will probably be open in a couple of days. They're taking cake samples and fingerprints—what else can they be doing?"

I shrugged. "Who knows! Perhaps having a big feast on my cupcakes back at the police station."

Thyme chuckled. "You're probably right. Anyway, I've heard the news."

I was momentarily alarmed. Did she mean that she knew I'd had lunch with Alder? "What news?" I said, somewhat defensively.

"You know, the news. Ruprecht translated some of the Latin text."

I breathed a sigh of relief. "Oh yes. He said it isn't necessarily an evil entity, but it might be."

Thyme patted me on the shoulder. "Why don't we go back to your place? Ruprecht wants us to make a list of suspects. Of course, he doesn't want us to speak to anyone or do anything. Just make lists, I suppose."

"Yes, we need to find out if the murderer was a human, because then we'll know what to do with the entity. Ruprecht said something about that. Come on home and we'll figure it out."

Thyme and I bought take-out coffee on the way, and Thyme insisted on getting take-out noodles. I didn't want to tell her that I just had lunch with Alder, so I would just have to try to eat the second lunch. I'd be horribly overweight if my friends didn't accept Alder any time soon.

It was a lovely sunny day, not too hot and not too cold. The only dark cloud in the sky was the murder of Scott Plank, so to speak.

As we walked up the front steps, the front door flew open. Thyme and I exchanged glances. I could hear the TV blaring, and walked into the living room. "Can you turn that off, or down?" Thyme asked me.

I shook my head. "No, the house is watching a *Game of Thrones* marathon. No spoilers by the way, or the house will get angry. It hasn't seen *Game of Thrones* before."

"It beats Jamie Oliver marathons," Thyme said, "as much as I like the man, although I do think you should've watched Jamie Oliver to improve your baking."

"I tried to do a spell for that," I said dryly, "and look how that turned out."

Just then, the house shook violently. Thyme clutched my arm. "What was that? Was it an earth tremor?"

I pointed to the TV. "No, the house does that every time somebody gets killed on *Game of Thrones*, and you know how often that happens! Oh look, now it's Jon Snow."

"But he…"

I put my finger to my mouth. "Shush! The house will get really angry if you mention any spoilers. Let's go to my altar room."

Thyme was clearly impressed. "You have an altar room now?"

I chuckled. "Yes, I figured that every Dark Witch needs an altar room."

"Don't you want to eat first?"

"I'm not hungry," I said truthfully.

I led Thyme to a small room next to the kitchen. The room was fairly bare, with just a small table, on which were several candles and crystals, sitting next to a computer desk, complete with a laptop.

"Well, that's a good start," Thyme said approvingly.

"The house made the room for me." I realized how weird that sounded after I'd said it, but the house could change rooms seemingly at will, and had created this extra room for me. It had a lovely view through a sash window over the side of the house that overlooked the paved area of the garden. It was a pretty view. Purple and white native violets grew wild from between the pavers, and scarlet coneflowers grew along the borders.

"It's much quieter in here," Thyme said.

I agreed. "The only thing is, I think the house wants the living room to itself." I turned on the computer. "Hang on a sec, I'll have to get you a chair." I soon returned with a kitchen chair and placed it next to my chair. "Do you want to fetch your food?"

"Let's write a list of suspects first," Thyme suggested.

"That won't take long." I typed: *Craig and Kayleen, entity*. I leaned back on my chair. "Surely there must be other suspects."

"Here, let me."

I pushed the laptop across to Thyme, and she searched Scott Plank's name. It brought up a long list of entries, most of them about the Council. Finally, Thyme flipped to *Google Images*. I gasped when I saw the top middle image. "There's a photo of Scott playing football with Craig!"

"But that doesn't mean anything, Amelia," Thyme said. "They were on the same team."

I shook my head. "I ran into Craig on my way to the shop just ten. I brought up the subject of Scott, and he insisted that he didn't know him."

Thyme tapped her chin. "Well now, that *is* interesting."

I thought it over for a moment. "Perhaps he only said that because I was asking questions. He was awfully defensive about it all."

Thyme opened a word document. "We need to make a To Do list. First of all, we have to ask around to see if Craig or Kayleen had anything against the victim. Then we need to ask around to see if anyone else had anything against the victim."

"Is that it?"

Thyme shrugged. "Can you think of anything else?"

The house rumbling again prevented me from answering. "George R.R. Martin must've done away with another character," I said. "No, I can't think of anything else. Any idea where to start asking?"

Thyme looked a little too pleased with herself. "I think it's about time you had a haircut."

I was puzzled. "What's that got to do with anything? Besides, I'm trying to let my hair grow. Last time I just wanted a trim, but the stylist cut off this much." I held my fingers apart to indicate the length.

Thyme did not look sympathetic. "Who knows everybody's business? Hairdressers, that's who! Call and make a booking and just bring up Scott Plank's name. You won't be able to stop the hairdresser talking."

I crossed my arms over my chest. "Why don't *you* go to the hairdresser and ask her?"

"I'm going to. There are three hair salons in town. I'll go to the one in the main street, and you can go to the one down that little lane right next to that café with the cranky owners."

"Thyme, my math is nowhere near as bad as my baking. Who's going to go to the third hairdresser? Camino or Mint?"

"No need. That hairdresser works from home, and she doesn't gossip at all. She's absolutely no use to us."

I turned my attention back to the laptop, hoping Thyme would forget that she wanted me to go to a hairdresser. I was trying to grow my hair, after all, and I didn't want to color it. I supposed I could go for a treatment. Finally, I uncovered something of interest. "Look, Thyme. The Council is having a wake for Scott tomorrow morning."

Thyme crossed to peer at the screen. "That's interesting," she said. "They say it's not a wake or a memorial service as such, but it's for his colleagues at the Council and all interested members of the community to pay their respects. It says all are welcome to attend."

I stood up and walked to the window to stretch my back. It had been improving considerably, but sitting still made it sore. "Why are they doing that?" I asked Thyme. "Why don't they just wait until the funeral?"

"Because the police will likely be hanging onto his body for too long," Thyme said. "I could take a week or two, possibly even longer, for the tests to come back. Don't forget, they're testing him for poisons."

"But wouldn't that be up to the family to hold a memorial service?"

Thyme shook her head. "The article stresses that it's not a memorial service as such. It's just some kind of a service to honor him."

"I wonder why the Council's doing that? I can't see how they'll make any money out of it."

"Oh Amelia, you've become so cynical! I have no idea why they're doing it, but one thing's for sure, we have to go."

I groaned. "But it will be all full of speeches, and really long boring ones at that. You know how I hate being bored."

Thyme stood up and put her hands on her hips. "You said yourself that the shop won't be open tomorrow, but it will probably be open the day after, so tomorrow will be our last good chance to snoop. Besides, don't they always say that the murderer goes to the victim's funeral?"

"But this isn't a funeral, it's just some sort of service in his honor," I protested.

"Good enough," Thyme said firmly.

Chapter 9

I was struck by the musty smell of the old Council Chambers building as soon as I walked through the door. I was sure I could smell the boredom, too.

Ruprecht, Camino, Mint, and of course Thyme had accompanied me. I wished I had downloaded a book onto my smart phone so I could read it when they were making the long, boring speeches which I was sure were to come.

We were ushered into a large room at the back of the building, declining to take one of the offered pamphlets about the allegedly fabulous upgrades to trash disposal and how that caused Council to double property taxes. We sat in the back row so we could have a good view of everyone. There were huge photos of Scott Plank placed at intervals around the walls. One would have thought he had been some sort of hero. Still, I suppose Thyme was right—we did need more information on Scott, and this was the best place to find it.

A man stepped up to the stage. "Esteemed guests, fellow Councilors, ladies and gentlemen. Welcome to the Bayberry Creek Council Chambers today. I'm the Mayor, Councilor Baldwin," he said in a booming voice. He then adjusted the microphone, which squeaked loudly in protest. He started again. "Esteemed guests, fellow Councilors, ladies and gentlemen, welcome here today. We are having the service for our dearly loved Councilor Scott Plank in the old Council Chambers, simply because the official opening of the new building is only a matter of days away, and we didn't feel it appropriate to have Councilor Plank's Memorial Service there before the building had been officially opened, despite the fact we're already using the new building."

His voice droned on and on and I thought of pinching myself to stay awake. To distract myself, I looked around at the surroundings to try to find something of interest on which I could focus.

To my surprise, there was a coffin at the front, up on the stage. I pointed this out to Thyme.

"That's probably Laurence Burleigh's idea." Thyme looked around before saying any more. "He's worked for the Council for years. He always wanted to be the Town Planner. Well, he is *a* Town Planner, just not *the* Town Planner. He was Scott's assistant. Before you ask, no, I'm sure he didn't murder Scott just to get his job. I mean, who does that?"

I supposed people did murder others to get their jobs, so it didn't seem all that far fetched. "But why the coffin?"

Thyme shrugged. "Laurence is a flamboyant personality, you know, way over the top. He probably should've been in musical theater rather than working as a Town Planner."

I nodded. "Perhaps this service won't be so boring, after all."

Thyme laughed. "We're here for information gathering, Amelia, not to be entertained."

"But I want to be entertained," I said with a laugh.

The Mayor's long, droning speech mercifully came to an end. He was handing over to another Councilor. I elbowed Thyme in the ribs. "Are you sure this is a good idea? I can barely stay awake." I yawned in an exaggerated manner.

The other Councilor crossed the stage, and just as his hand reached out to the microphone from the Deputy Mayor, another man appeared. I did a double take. This man was brightly dressed in a red suit with a bright yellow waistcoat and green spotted tie. A top hat was perched on his head. Surely this must be the flamboyant Laurence Burleigh. The man took the microphone from the Deputy Mayor, who appeared to be stunned.

At that moment, there was a boom of thunder and the coffin lid slammed shut. The entire crowd jumped.

"Welcome to you all," the man said with a flourish. "No one wants a boring memorial service, so I'm here to sing the praises of Scott Plank. Whether those praises are actually deserved, I shall leave it up to you." With that, he raised his top hat, and tap danced halfway across the stage, before tap dancing back to the microphone and swinging his cane. He took the microphone, and then sang what appeared to be an impromptu song praising the victim.

I was stunned. I sat there, speechless, until Thyme leaned over to me. "Well, you *did* say you wanted to be entertained, Amelia."

It was then that it struck me. "Is that Laurence Burleigh?" I whispered back.

"No, no idea who he is."

"Thyme, I'm pretty sure that's the entity," I whispered urgently.

"Are you sure?"

I shook my head and then nodded. "No, but I'm pretty sure."

Ruprecht, who was sitting next to Thyme, leaned over. "That's him?"

I nodded. "I think so. I *did* say I wanted to be entertained."

Ruprecht stroked his chain for a while before answering. "Yes, there was too much of a magical vibe around the man. I suspected at once that the man was, in fact, a supernatural being, but I couldn't bring myself to believe it. And you said you wished to be entertained? He must be carrying out your wishes. Are you aware of the legend of the genie? The origins, I mean?"

Mint tapped him on the shoulder. "Grandfather, I don't think this is the time to give Amelia a history lesson."

Ruprecht appeared to be deciding between Mint's words and his desire to give me said history lesson. "Amelia, this entity is carrying out your wishes. Be very careful what you wish for from now on, until we find a way to deal with it."

I was aghast. "How will I be able to control my thoughts?" I figured it would be like one of my many attempts at meditation. Anything I try not to focus on, I invariably focus on.

Ruprecht shook his head. "You don't need to worry, it's only if you wish aloud. The entity can't read your mind, so it can only obey your spoken wishes. Let me amend that, it will only do what it *thinks* are your spoken wishes."

I sank down in the chair with a sigh of relief. "Thank goodness! He didn't kill that man after all."

My relief was to be short lived. Ruprecht leaned over once more. "Amelia, are you sure you didn't say you wanted to kill Scott?"

I was horrified. "Of course I didn't!"

Ruprecht frowned. "You told me that Scott threw a cupcake on your floor. When you walked away, did you mutter anything to yourself like, 'I'd like to kill him,' or words to that effect?"

All the blood drained from my face.

Chapter 10

The entity finished his speech, and then handed the microphone over to an actual Councilor, who at once commenced a boring speech in a monotone. This time, I didn't mind. I was glad to be surrounded by boredom while I tried to collect my thoughts. Had I muttered that I'd like to kill Scott Plank? I didn't recall doing so, but then again, it was entirely possible.

By the end of the speech, I had come to the conclusion that there was nothing I could do about the entity, not right now. Ruprecht would have to be the one to dispatch it. It was still possible, even likely, that Scott was murdered by a human. I had to look into that option, and this service was the best place to do it. I knew that people would mingle after the service, and so we were likely to be mingling with the murderer. Then again, detectives might arrest someone in the next few days, with any luck. I tried to force myself to feel optimistic.

My phone vibrated, and I pulled it from my pocket. It was an incoming call from a number I didn't recognize. I whispered to Thyme, "I have to take this," and hurried outside.

It was Detective Greene. "Miss Spelled, we're finished with your store now. You're free to return."

With that, he hung up. While I was pleased I could return to my store, I was puzzled that he hadn't said more. It would have been good if he had let on whether or not he thought I was a suspect, or whether he had information on the case.

Once I was outside, I had a wicked urge to go and get coffee and then return when the service was over, but I resisted my bad self and went back inside.

Two hours later, the service was drawing to a close. Everyone was yawning, whether from the lack of oxygen in the musty building or from sheer boredom, I had no idea.

I stood up, and then realized that my back had stopped hurting. Well, that was something to be grateful for. I turned around and saw Mint shaking Camino gently. She had been snoring, although I had mistaken the sound for the noise of the ceiling fan.

The five of us walked over to the refreshments table, where chocolate cookies, plain cookies, and two urns filled with hot water along with jars of instant coffee and packets of teabags, filled every available surface. I eyed the instant coffee with alarm.

"Low budget," Thyme said to me. "They must've spent all their money on catering for the new building. Well, our offering will be vastly better than this."

Ruprecht spoke from behind us. "You two split up. Go and mingle, and Mint, Camino and I will likewise mingle, and then we'll meet up later and compare notes. Remember, we're looking for anyone who had a grudge against Scott."

Thyme and I nodded. Thyme stuffed a chocolate cookie in her mouth, and made to go into the crowd, when I caught her arm. "Let's stay around here. Everyone will be coming here at some point."

"Good idea." Thyme selected another cookie.

Helen Harden, the physical therapist, hurried over to me. "Hello Amelia, how's your back? I hope you weren't sitting there all this time?"

I felt a little guilty. "Yes, I was, but my back's been good all day. In fact, I'd completely forgotten about it."

Helen bit her lip. "Well that's good, but don't take it lightly. You need to keep doing the exercises I showed you and perhaps make another appointment. And remember, try not to sit for long periods at a time. Anyway, enough talking shop. This is my husband, Henry."

Henry and I shook hands. He had a particularly strong grip. "Yes, I know you from the cake store," he said.

I gestured to Thyme. "This is my friend, Thyme," I said to Helen, because Thyme and Henry would have recognized each other from the cake shop. He was a fairly regular customer.

"Did you know Mr. Plank well?" Thyme asked them.

Helen snorted rudely. "Yes, but not in a good way. I don't know why we're here, but Henry insisted we come. I don't mean to speak ill of the dead, but Scott Plank cheated us over a big real estate deal."

Henry shot his wife a withering look, and then abruptly changed the subject. "That was a rather strange memorial service, wasn't it? I have no idea who that tap dancing man was."

We all laughed politely.

Henry grabbed his wife's arm and ushered her away. I overheard Helen whisper, "I didn't go into detail! There was nothing wrong with saying that."

Thyme raised her eyebrows. "Well, that didn't take us long at all, did it? We can add Henry and Helen Harden to the list of suspects."

I had to agree. "Yes, and did you see how awkward he looked when she mentioned that Scott cheated them in a property deal? We have to find out how long ago that was."

"Good idea," Thyme said. "If it was ten years ago, then that won't be significant, but if it was recent, then it could be significant. Of course, the police must already know this."

"Oh that reminds me. That call I got, when I left the service, was from the detectives. They said we're allowed back in the shop now."

"That's a relief!" Thyme popped a cookie into her mouth. "You know, Scott was the Town Planner, and if he cheated Henry and Helen, then it was likely that he cheated others. I think we're onto something here."

I nodded. "I only hope that they don't cancel the catering for the opening of the Council Chambers, given that Scott was murdered in my store and all."

Thyme bit her lip, but didn't reply. I was about to say more to her, when the woman who had booked me for the catering caught my eye and hurried over to me. I held my breath. She launched straight into speech. "Amelia and Thyme, good to see you both here. I must apologize. Obviously, we didn't cater this. The Mayor just sent people out for tea, coffee, and cookies." Her tone was apologetic, and I was relieved. She didn't appear to have any intention of canceling the catering. "So we're on schedule for the opening?"

I nodded. "Yes," I said. "I assume it's still going ahead on time, despite what happened to Scott Plank?"

A scowl crossed the woman's face. "Of course. I don't think you'll see too many people mourning over that pig of a man." Her cheeks flushed red with either embarrassment or anger. She excused herself and hurried away.

"Phew! What a relief," I said to Thyme.

"It sure is. Amelia, do we have to add her to our list of suspects, too? I mean, did everyone hate the man?"

I shrugged. "It's only two suspects so far, if you count Helen and her husband as joint suspects."

"Two out of two," Thyme pointed out. "That's one hundred percent."

"But not a viable statistic," I said. "Only two suspects after all."

Thyme clutched my arm, and nodded to a man nearby. I figured he was Laurence Burleigh. After all, he was dressed brightly, although not quite as brightly as the entity, who, by the way, I hadn't seen since his speech. He was talking to another man, and Scott Plank's name was mentioned. Thyme and I edged closer.

"So you'll be the Town Planner now, Laurence?" the shorter man said.

"Yes, that's right."

The other man extended his hand and shook Laurence's vigorously. "What a relief! That will end some of the corruption on the Council."

"I hope it ends *all* the corruption on the Council," Laurence said firmly.

"I'm sorry he's dead," the short man continued, "as far as I care about any human being that's been murdered. I mean, you wouldn't wish that on your worst enemy, but Scott Plank was a blight on humanity."

"You won't get any argument from me," Laurence said. At that point, the two men looked at us, so I avoided eye contact and selected a cookie. Thyme did the same. I went to the other end of the table, and Thyme followed me.

"The suspects list is getting rather long," I said in a low voice.

Thyme chuckled. "Still a small number of people, four, but that's four out of four. Still one hundred percent."

I resisted the urge to throw a piece of my cookie at her. "Have you seen the entity at all? We should keep an eye out for him."

Thyme shook her head. "No, I haven't seen anything unusual. Perhaps you should make a wish aloud, and see what he does."

"No way! I'll only do that under controlled conditions, with Ruprecht there. And speaking of Ruprecht, I wonder how he, Camino, and Mint are going with gathering information?"

"We should all go to Ruprecht's for dinner tonight and discuss it."

I figured now was as good a time as any to break the news. "Thyme, I'm going over to Alder's for dinner tonight." Thyme did not look happy so I hurried to add, "We're going to look through his family's old books and see if there's anything about the entity."

Thyme raised her eyebrows. "Is that like asking you up to see his etchings?"

I pulled a face. "Ha ha, very funny. Thyme, I know you don't like Alder, but I really do. He really isn't like his family. He doesn't have anything against witches at all."

"Look Amelia, I respect your wishes, but don't expect me to like him."

I supposed that was fair enough. "At least his family has all those ancient books, so that might turn up something about the entity."

"I suppose so," Thyme said after she finished another cookie. "But it would be good if you could find out the type of entity it is or even its name."

I agreed. "I wish I knew its name."

Thyme clapped her hand over her mouth, and I realized too late that I had wished aloud. Someone tapped me on the shoulder. I turned around, and there was a man standing behind me. "My name is Fred."

"Fred?" I said.

"What's wrong with my name?" the man said defensively. "It's a good solid name. I supposed you expected me to have a magical name like Callakazam! I think you've been watching too many movies." With that, he spun on his heel and walked away in an obvious huff.

I turned to Thyme, but the Mayor hurried over to me, followed by a man in a tight suit. "Did you enjoy the service, Miss Spelled?"

"Yes," I lied. "You spoke beautifully about Mr. Plank."

The Mayor rubbed at his dry eyes and sniffed. "Excuse me, I'm so emotional. Yes, dear Scott was wonderful, wonderful! He will be sorely missed. Isn't that right, Cedric?"

The man in the tight suit forced a smile. "Wonderful," he said in a choked voice.

The Mayor hurried away to speak to someone else, followed by the unfortunate Cedric. Two elderly ladies who had lamingtons piled on their paper plates scoffed loudly. "*Wonderful*? Did you hear that, Myrtle? What a joke!"

"Yes, Beatrice, he was an evil man, evil. Oh Mr. Foxtin-Flynn, how are you today?"

Ruprecht kissed both ladies' hands. "Better for seeing you, my dear ladies."

The ladies twittered nervously before sitting on the nearest chairs and continuing their conversation.

Ruprecht came straight to the point. "Did you find out any information?"

"Just that the Mayor is the only one with a good word about the deceased," I said. "Everyone else hated him."

Thyme nudged me in the ribs. "Amelia! How could you forget? The entity's name is Fred."

Mint and Camino chuckled. "Are you serious?" Mint asked. "I thought his name would be Belphegor or Ziminiar."

"Or Sejazel or Eisheth," Camino added with a laugh.

I held up my hands. "What can I say?" I noticed that Ruprecht was not joining in the laughter. "I'm sorry to say that I wished I knew his name."

Ruprecht nodded solemnly. "I was afraid as much. Try to be careful with your words, Amelia."

I nodded, suitably chastened. "Helen Harden did let slip that Scott cheated them—her husband wasn't happy that she said that, either—and then everyone we spoke to was full of venom about Scott. Even those two ladies didn't like him."

Ruprecht clasped his hands. "I'm afraid an obvious suspect hasn't come to the fore."

I knew what Ruprecht was thinking but was too kind to say. The entity was the main suspect, and since I had summoned him, I was responsible for a man's death.

Chapter 11

I caught my heel in the cobblestones and, after flailing my arms wildly, paused to compose myself. No one had seen me recover from the face plant, as the little side street was invariably deserted at any time of day. Ahead I could see the entrance to Alder's office—hard to miss given the impressive gothic wrought iron bars covering the windows.

I had that awful nervous feeling one gets before entering some sort of competition, such as a race. When I reached the heavy oak door, I rested my hand on the brass handle and took a deep breath. *Here goes!* I rang the bell. As I waited for Alder to answer the door, I looked up and forced myself to focus on the bottle green awning and the pretty blue-green porch ceiling.

When Alder opened the door, I at once noticed the scent of lemongrass and citronella. "Van Van Oil?" I asked him, and then instantly regretted my opening words.

"Amelia, come in." Alder stood aside for me to enter. "Yes, I did a floor wash earlier."

"Because of Fred? Oh, that's the entity's name. I wished he'd tell me what his name was, and he did." I silently scolded myself. *Stop talking, you idiot. Take a deep breath.*

I've never seen Alder look so shocked. "Fred? You're kidding me, right?"

I was still standing in his doorway. "That's what he said his name was, and he didn't appear to be joking."

The corners of Alder's mouth twitched. "I don't think you'll be able to banish him then, because I'm sure the family's ancient spell books don't have any mention of an entity by the name of Fred." Alder put his hand under my elbow and steered me inside.

I hoped Alder couldn't see my knees shaking. To say I was nervous about the upcoming dinner was an understatement. Alder had never kissed me, and it wasn't as if we were officially dating. The very thought made my heart race, and I shivered.

Luckily, Alder had his back to me and couldn't see my discomfort. He ushered me down the long corridor past his office entrance and into his private apartment at the back of the building. It was still daylight, and the dimming sunlight fell gently on the flowers in the high walled garden. I could almost smell the honeysuckle trailing over the high brick walls. I forced my attention from the bi-fold doors back to the kitchen.

I cast my eyes around the industrial chic, stainless steel and utterly spotless kitchen and realized that Alder was likely a neat-freak, but I could forgive him that flaw. He nodded to his dining table and pulled out a chair for me. "Sit down and relax while I finish dinner." He poured me a glass of wine. "Chardonnay."

I was touched that he remembered I was partial to Chardonnay. Of course, it was hard to relax with Alder in front of me. After all, he was tall, incredibly good looking, with a wicked and mysterious edge. Alder caught my eye and winked at me. I pushed my heels into the floor to stop my knees shaking. "So, tell me more about this Fred." He chuckled as he said it.

"*This Fred* could be a murderer," I pointed out.

"I doubt it." Alder turned to the wok over the gas flame before speaking again. "Scott Plank wasn't at all popular, and he was involved in some shady deals. I'd be very surprised if he wasn't murdered by a real, live human."

"I hope so," I said fervently, immediately followed by, "Oh, that didn't sound good. Of course, I'm sorry that he was murdered, but I just don't want to be the one responsible for it."

Alder nodded. "That's entirely understandable. Have you come up with any suspects yet?"

I spun my glass of wine around. "No, but I went to his memorial service earlier today, and there wasn't a single person there with a good word to say about him. Well, apart from the usual platitudes you'd expect at that sort of thing, and even those were few and far between."

Alder looked up from his preparations and smiled at me. "After dinner, we'll look through the books and see what we can find. I hope you like *nasi goreng istimewa?*"

"Yes," I said. I, in fact, had not the slightest clue what the dish was, but it sure smelled good. I started to relax as Alder stirred the wok. He had cooked Thai green pumpkin curry on the only other occasion I'd been in his apartment, an impromptu dinner that time. I liked the faint smell of gas emanating from his gas stovetop—it reminded me of those few occasions I had gone camping with my parents as a young child. Of course, the only things that emanated from stovetops when I cooked were thick black smoke and hideously charred remains.

I took the opportunity to study Alder. He was dark and brooding. I didn't like sulky men, but Alder didn't have that type of energy at all.

"So, how are you adjusting to being a Dark Witch?"

I jumped. "I'm still adjusting to being any sort of witch," I said with a laugh. "There's so much to learn, you know, spells, herbs, potions, and all that."

"I could give you lessons."

I'll bet you could, I thought, and then fervently hoped Alder didn't know what I was thinking.

Apparently, Alder wasn't a mind reader, and he continued speaking without pause. "Magic comes from within," he said with a flourish of his wooden spoon.

"You sound like Ruprecht," I said.

Alder flashed me a look before continuing. "If you can visualize and concentrate, then you can do magic. It's really that simple. All the potions and spells in the world won't help someone who can't focus. Some people follow the inner temple tradition. To put it simply, someone can visualize all their ritual workings in a visual temple." I must have shown my confusion, as he continued. "Say you are somewhere and you want to do a spell for say, communication, but you cannot because of your location. Perhaps you are visiting friends, for example, and can't just whip out a candle and perform a spell. So then, you go into your inner temple in your mind's eye. You visualize a yellow candle there and you visualize the spell. That works just as well as a spell carried about with an actual candle. Do you understand?"

I nodded. "Yes, it makes sense. What a good idea." To be honest, I was having trouble concentrating, because, well, Alder was there.

The topic on witchcraft continued over dinner. While I found it interesting, I was a little saddened by this, because I'd hoped it would be somewhat romantic.

Alder was still talking about witchcraft when he cleared the table and asked me if I'd like dessert.

"Do you like baked white chocolate cheesecake with raspberries?" he asked.

"Do I ever!" I exclaimed. "Would you like some help with it?"

A look of fear crossed his face. "No, it's fine! Thanks anyway." He held up a hand as if to keep me away from the kitchen. Wise, as well as good looking. What more could a girl want?

The dessert was delicious. When we finished, Alder cleared the table, again refusing my offer of help. "And let's do what you've wanted to do all evening!" he exclaimed.

I felt my cheeks burn. Surely he didn't mean…?

"My ancient books!"

"Oh!" I was mortally embarrassed. I hoped Alder hadn't noticed my discomfort. I looked away, and focused on the leg of a chair.

Alder indicated I should follow him, and so I did, my ears burning and my face burning. He opened the door and I gasped with delight. Whereas the rest of the house was minimalist industrial, this room was everything but. There were shelves and shelves of ancient looking, leather-bound books, all stored flat and not upright.

I caught a glimpse of myself in the heavy gilt mirror at the end of the room, and looked away quickly. My face was indeed bright red.

Alder shut the door. "Temperature and humidity control," he explained. "These are old, rare books." He threw me a pair of white gloves and I only just caught them.

I walked along the shelves and looked at some titles: *Sworn Book of Honorius*, *The Magus*, *A New and Complete Illustration of the Celestial Science of Astrology*, *The Fourth Book of Occult Philosophy*, and so it went on.

Alder carefully opened two books on the table in the center of the room. "These two are most likely. Let's look through one each."

I couldn't find anything that would help, although the information was fascinating. I lost myself in reading about various hideous demons and their characteristics.

Alder's voice broke me from my reverie. "Amelia, what did Ruprecht say the spelling mistake was?"

I tried to remember. "No, he didn't say precisely, and he said there could be more. Why?"

"I think Fred is a haint. Have a look at this illustration."

I leaned close to Alder and looked at the drawing. Sure enough, the apparition looked just as

Fred had, when he had first appeared to me. "He looks like a haint, all right. Do haints grant wishes?"

Alder shook his head, and seemed amused by my comment. "No, but you were doing a spell to improve your baking, weren't you?" I nodded. "So it seems you have summoned a haint to help you. Perhaps that's why it's trying to grant your wishes. You're a Dark Witch and that's why you have control over it to some degree."

"What *is* a haint?"

Alder looked worried momentarily. "The word originated with the Gullah people in Africa, and referred to evil spirits. After that, the word became confused with 'haunts,' so these days, people get the two mixed up."

"I'm not sure I'm following you," I said.

"Bottom line, it's either evil spirits or spirits of the dead," Adler said. "No one knows for sure."

"Spirits of the dead, as in ghosts?"

Alder nodded. "The thing is, many people confuse the word 'haints' with the word 'haunts,' and that confuses the origin. It led to haints being thought of as ghosts, specifically, restless ghosts who haven't been able to pass over for whatever reason. Either way, it's not something you'd want. The tradition carried into the south of the USA, where many people take protective measures against haints."

"But haints are everywhere?"

Alder shrugged. "Most likely. They're not limited to one culture or one geographical area, as far as I'm aware. They have different names, but they're the same entity. Coffee? We can head back out to the kitchen and discuss it."

As we left the room, I excused myself to go to the bathroom. I was saddened, as I was beginning to think that Alder wasn't interested in me in a romantic way. All he had talked about all night was witchcraft. "I wish he'd kiss me," I said to my reflection. "He just doesn't seem interested in me at all. Maybe he just wants to be friends because we're both Dark Witches! How silly could I be!"

I walked back out to the kitchen, crestfallen. I hadn't quite reached the table when I felt a gentle hand on my shoulder. Alder spun me around to face him. "I've wanted to do this since I first met you," Alder said, pulling me close.

The next thing I knew, his lips were on mine, gentle yet insistent. I fervently kissed him back, not caring for the moment that Fred was making him do this. I wasn't thinking about Fred—I was thinking that Alder was an amazing kisser as I melted into him, savoring the taste of his lips.

Alder's phone rang, and we both jumped. He broke away and briefly looked at the screen. "Sorry, Amelia. I have to take this." He abruptly took the phone out of the room. I just stood there, feeling awkward.

Alder soon returned. "Sorry about this," he said once more. "This is confidential." I nodded. "It's a new client, Penny Plank."

"Plank?" I echoed. "A relative of the victim's?"

"His ex-wife. She's in town and I have to meet her right now. I'm sorry that I can't go into the details. I'll drive you home."

I tried not to let my disappointment show, but I told myself that it was probably for the best. If Fred had influenced Alder to kiss me—and I was fairly certain that he had—then I had no right kissing someone who wouldn't have any intention of kissing me when he was in his right mind.

Chapter 12

I thought the night couldn't get any worse. As Alder's car pulled up outside my home, much to my dismay I saw Ruprecht, Thyme, and Mint getting out of Ruprecht's car outside Camino's house, which of course, was next door to my house.

Their jaws all dropped when they saw me emerge from Alder's car. I mumbled my goodbyes to Alder and walked over to them, feeling awfully guilty and at the same time, annoyed for myself for feeling guilty. Alder had not so long ago confided in me that he was a Dark Witch too, and while he had asked me not to tell the others, he had also said I could tell them if I really wanted to do so. I felt in an awkward position, keeping Alder's secret from my friends.

"Amelia, good to see you," Ruprecht said, obviously in an attempt to relieve the tension. "Come inside to Camino's. We have new information." I saw he was clutching the Book of Shadows to him.

"This is a surprise," Thyme whispered to me as we walked in behind the others.

"You knew I was having dinner with Alder."

Thyme winked at me. "I didn't expect you'd be back so soon."

I frowned at her. Oh well, I suppose being teased wasn't as bad as her acting weird that I was with Alder. I chose to remain silent.

Ruprecht knocked once and then turned to me. "I'm returning your Great Aunt Thelma's Book of Shadows to you."

"Thelma couldn't have foreseen that I'd summon a spirit," I said sadly, just as Camino opened the door. She was dressed as a giant, olive-brown, spotted toad. I squealed, while the others, even the usually unflappable Ruprecht, gasped.

"Is that a new onesie, Camino?" Ruprecht asked her.

Camino twirled like a ballet dancer, as far as one could tell given that she was dressed as a toad. "Do you like it?" she asked proudly through the huge mouth. "It's a cane toad onesie."

Everyone nodded, although far from enthusiastically. "Um, aren't cane toads very dangerous, like, um, venomous?" I asked her. I recoiled from the enormous fake warts on the suit.

Camino laughed. "Exactly! You don't mess with them! Oh, I don't spit poison, by the way."

Well, that was reassuring. We all hurried past Camino into her living room. Camino's house always made me feel like I was stepping back in time, entering another era. The old-fashioned and drab furniture was nevertheless enlivened by the countless candles placed around the room, and the arcane fragrances that emanated from them.

Camino indicated we should all sit. As she did so, she fell backward over a chair, and her webbed feet pitched skyward. The nearest candles quivered, sending a ripple of shadows across the walls. Mint struggled to right her while Ruprecht averted his eyes.

"Now to business," Ruprecht said when the toad was sitting comfortably. "Amelia, while you were, err, away, we made a list of suspects. We have Fred, Craig and Kayleen, Laurence Burleigh, and Penny Plank. It's not a hard and fast list, by any means, but it's a start."

I had pricked up my ears at the mention of Penny Plank. "I know the others, but I've never met Penny Plank."

"She's Scott's ex-wife," Ruprecht explained, but I already knew that.

"Does she live in town?" I asked him.

Ruprecht shook his head. "She hasn't been in town for years, and she wasn't at the memorial service this morning, but Camino saw her in town today."

Thyme spoke up. "Are you sure it was her?"

Camino nodded. At least, I think that's what she was doing. It was hard to tell, given that she was ensconced in a deadly toad suit. "I saw her coming out of the police station late this afternoon, and she didn't look happy."

"Well, perhaps the detectives called her in for questioning," I said. "That's not suspicious in itself, is it?"

Ruprecht looked solemn. "She lives in Port Macquarie, actually. That's a few hours' drive from here. I *do* find it suspicious that she just happened to be in town when her ex-husband was murdered, given that I haven't seen her here for years. No doubt, the police would share my view."

"Yes, that certainly does seem fishy," I said. "But if they have children, then perhaps she was here for something to do with them."

"It's entirely possible," Ruprecht admitted. "We'll need to find out if she's here with their children, and if there's some sporting event or suchlike that they might be attending. If not, then I find her presence in town rather suspicious."

"What about Laurence Burleigh?" Mint asked. "He takes over Scott's job, and I heard it'll be a permanent position. The Mayor himself told me that they won't be advertising it. That's a huge jump in pay. Still, it seems like a tenuous motive."

"Perhaps Laurence had a different reason for wanting to kill Scott," I said. "He was full of venom when he mentioned Scott this morning. Ruprecht, I can't say that I w-i-s-h that the murderer will be revealed, can I? Then the entity will reveal it."

Thyme chuckled. "I wondered why you spelled the word."

I shrugged. "Just to be on the safe side."

Ruprecht held up one finger. "No, Amelia, that would be the worst thing you could do. You need to remove that word from your vocabulary for the time being."

Camino pulled off her cane toad head. It left every last piece of her hair sticking skyward. I did my best not to laugh. "I was suffocating under there," she said sadly. "I won't be able to sleep in it. I should've bought that long-nosed bandicoot onesie when I saw it online the other day. It should be much more comfortable to sleep in. I'll buy you one too, Amelia, for your birthday.'

"That's so kind of you, but my birthday isn't for a long time," I said hopefully. "A *very* long time."

Camino waved my concerns away. "So you haven't seen Fred again recently?"

"No, he hasn't been around since this morning." At least, I hoped that was the case. Had Fred in fact made Alder kiss me? I was fairly certain he had, but I had to put that out of my mind for the minute. "Ruprecht, have you made any progress on finding out anything about Fred?"

He shook his head. "Sadly, I haven't. Summoning is always easy, even for the most unskilled or novice person, but banishing a spirit is quite another matter."

I took a deep breath. "Alder showed me his collection of witchcraft books. After what we read, we think that Fred is a haint. Ruprecht, is there any chance that the word 'haint' appears as a spelling mistake in the text, in addition to the error you found?"

Ruprecht hurried to his feet. "Let's have a look." He carried the book to Camino's dining room table, where he opened it.

Ruprecht took an awfully long time poring over the Book of Shadows, even by his standards. After what seemed an age, he jabbed his finger at the book. "There! That word there should be *aiunt*, Latin third person plural active indicative of the verb *aio*, 'I affirm.'"

"Sorry, I didn't understand a word of that," I admitted. By the looks on the others' faces, they didn't either.

"In a nutshell, the word should be *aiunt*, meaning 'they affirm,' but instead it is *haint*. Granted, one is a verb and one is a noun, but I can explain the syntax of the sentence to you in detail."

Mercifully, Camino prevented him. "No, none of us would understand you, if I'm honest," she said quickly. "Are you saying that Amelia has summoned a haint?"

Ruprecht nodded solemnly.

"That's not good, right?" I said. "So Fred's a haint?"

Ruprecht nodded again. "Yes, he's a haint, and no, it is not good. Far from it."

"How do we get rid of him?" was my next question.

"I don't know. I'm not aware of anyone banishing a haint, simply protecting oneself from one, warding one off."

"How?" we all said at once.

"Traditionally by the color blue. Haints are supposed to have an aversion to the color. Have you ever seen those Southern homes where the porch ceilings are painted a pretty blue-green or light blue?" He looked at each of us in turn, and then pressed on. "That color is known as 'haint blue.' It's supposed to keep haints away."

"Why?" I asked him.

Ruprecht shut the Book of Shadows. "No one knows. Some legends say that haints won't cross seawater, but no one really knows for sure. I'm afraid that knowing Fred is a haint brings us no closer to knowing whether or not he was the murderer."

Silence settled over the room. "I should light some lemongrass incense," Camino said, "or perhaps some asafoetida."

Thyme pulled a face. "Lemongrass would be better. Asafoetida smells absolutely disgusting. They don't call it 'devil's dung' for nothing."

"Let me light the incense, Camino," Mint said. "If the fire gets too close to your onesie, you'll go up in smoke."

Ruprecht turned to look at me. "Amelia, you'll have to banish the haint."

"Me?" I squeaked. "But how?"

"I'm afraid that's something you'll have to figure out for yourself." Ruprecht's tone was solemn. "You're a Dark Witch, and now is the time for you to recognize your powers and act on them."

The rest of the evening was somewhat of a blur. I tossed and turned in bed that night, unable to sleep, burdened with worries. Had the haint killed Scott Plank? And had it made Alder kiss me? A selfish thought, I know, given the gravity of the situation, but one I just couldn't get out of my mind. And worst of all, how would I be able to come into my powers as a Dark Witch? I didn't even know what that entailed.

Willow and Hawthorn swiped at me as I rolled over in bed once more, annoyed I had disturbed them from their resting place on top of my legs.

Willow walked up to my face to glare at me. "What am I going to do, Willow?" Of course, there was no reply, so I tried once more to fall asleep.

Chapter 13

I woke up to the sound of yet another strident battle. The house was up early this morning. Rubbing my eyes, I staggered into the living room to turn off the TV. "Please just let me have coffee first," I said to the house.

Willow and Hawthorn had followed me every step of the way, complaining loudly that I had the nerve to do something other than feed them the second my eyes had opened. I went back into my usual routine, switching on the coffee and then filling the cats' bowls with food.

I slumped over the coffee machine and waited for it to do its magic, figuratively speaking. That sound was my favorite sound in the world. Soon, the first hit of caffeine was oozing delightfully through my body. I took up my cup and went back into the living room, where I opened the curtains. To my alarm, I saw Kayleen's van parked at my front gate. What was she doing here? I had gone to the expense of getting a Post Office Box just to make sure Kayleen never darkened my doorstep again.

I watched as she walked toward my iron gate, resting her hands on it. I set down my coffee cup, wrapped my bathrobe around me tightly, and hurried down the front path.

"Parcel!" Kayleen barked.

"What? I have a Post Office Box now. I'm not supposed to get any mail here."

"Maybe you should get a redirection order," Kayleen said in a snide tone.

"I *do* have one, a two-year one," I said.

Kayleen snickered. "Perhaps *someone* at the Post Office forgot to put on the redirection sticker."

I crossed my arms and took a shallow breath. Her extravagantly applied and cheap floral perfume was tickling my nose. "Like I said, I'm not supposed to get any mail here. That's why I paid all that money for a Post Office Box. They're not cheap, you know." I was exasperated.

Kayleen thrust a small parcel at me by way of response. "You're a witch!"

I was taken aback. "Excuse me?" I snatched the parcel from her.

"You heard me!" Kayleen thrust out her jaw in a belligerent manner. "There's protection incense in there. Only witches use protection incense."

"You opened my package!" I said accusingly. I could see that only part of the yellow and red sealed tape was still on the package, and someone had hastily covered it over with clear adhesive tape.

"The outside says *Nightfilled Witch Supply Shop*," Kayleen said, leaning over me and jabbing her stubby finger at the package.

"But it doesn't say what's *inside* the package. It's illegal to open people's mail, Kayleen."

Kayleen smirked at me. "Well, what are you going to do about it, Amelia? Australia Post gets complaints like that all the time. They won't do anything about it. Trust me, I know." Her eyes narrowed into slits.

I was furious. "We've spoken about this before, Kayleen. You say that I'm a witch, so do you think it's wise to be so nasty to a witch?"

Kayleen hesitated. "What are you going to do about it then, Miss Smarty Pants?" Her belligerent manner had, however, lost some of its sting.

"I've already told you that I'll turn you into a toad." It was the best I could come up with, and the last time I'd said that to her, she had seemed somewhat frightened.

"Craig says it's impossible to turn someone into a toad. Anyway, you're just jealous that I'm dating Craig. You wanted him for yourself. Keep your hands off him. He's all mine!"

I shook my head. "You can have him." Just then, out of my peripheral vision, I saw Camino heading for Kayleen. I figured she must be expecting a package. Camino was dressed in her cane toad onesie. It couldn't be more perfect.

"Yes, Kayleen, you're right. I *am* a witch, and I *will* turn you into a toad. I've been practicing. My neighbor annoyed me, so I turned her into a toad."

Kayleen snorted. "Oh Amelia, you're so full of…" She stopped speaking when she saw Camino, a.k.a. a giant cane toad, hopping quickly down toward her.

Kayleen threw her arms in the air, let out a bloodcurdling scream, and sprinted for her van. Within seconds, she was out of sight. I had no idea that old van could go so fast.

Camino lifted off her cane toad head. "Oh no, I was expecting a package today. I was hoping to catch that dreadful woman, because she always cards me."

After that scene with Kayleen, I had five cups of coffee before I headed for the store. Kayleen had shaken me up, but I don't know why I thought coffee would help. I was wide awake, but not at all calm. I figured things were about to get worse when I saw Sergeant Tinsdell and Constable Dawson waiting for me at the front door of my store.

I saw at once that Tinsdell looked a bit sheepish, not his usual self. "Can we speak to you, Miss Spelled?"

"Sure." I unlocked the door, and they followed me inside the shop.

"Is Miss Thyme working here today?" Constable Dawson asked, a little too eagerly.

"Yes, she'll be here in about five minutes or so," I said. "What can I do for you?"

Tinsdell shuffled from one foot to another. "We're obliged to follow up all complaints."

I nodded, wondering where he was going with this.

"Someone has lodged a complaint against you. She said you threatened her."

I raised my eyebrows. "Kayleen! Threatened her with what, exactly?"

Sergeant Tinsdell looked over in the direction of the lemon cheesecake cupcakes. "Um, she said you threatened to turn her into a toad."

I put my hands on my hips. "Yes, I did. I'm sure that's not against the law, is it?" I said through gritted teeth. "She brought a package to my house, despite the fact I have a Post Office Box and she accused me of being a witch. I can't believe you actually came here over this."

Tinsdell had the grace to look embarrassed. "Like I said, Miss Spelled, we have to follow up all claims of threats, no matter how, um, far-fetched those threats might be."

"And don't forget, Craig and Kayleen were in the shop with the victim when I left to go to the kitchen. I wasn't gone long at all, and when I came back, Scott Plank was lying strangled on the ground. I didn't see anyone else around."

"Yes, Miss Spelled. That's a matter of record. Are you saying you believe those two murdered him?"

I shook my head. "I actually don't have a clue who murdered him. I'm just saying that I think it's strange that the three of them were in the shop together; I left for a short time, and when I came back, they were missing and he was dead. I told the detectives that. It's all in my statement."

"Well, thanks for your help, Miss Spelled." With that, Tinsdell headed for the door, followed by Constable Dawson who was looking around him hopefully, no doubt for Thyme.

Thyme arrived five minutes later. I was smudging the shop with white sage—after all, a man had been murdered in there—and I quickly brought her up to speed with the day's events. She doubled over laughing about Camino, the giant cane toad, hopping toward Kayleen, but sobered up quickly to discover she had missed Constable Dawson.

"What can we do to investigate Craig?" I asked her. "He had the opportunity, but what motive did he have?"

"Or what motive did Kayleen have? If either of them did it, then they had to be in it together," Thyme pointed out.

I washed my hands and then dried them. "Sure, but what motive did Kayleen have? I don't know where to start investigating those two."

Thyme slapped her forehead. "Silly me, the hairdresser!"

I groaned. How could I have forgotten that?

Thyme continued gleefully, "Call both hairdressers and see if you can get an appointment right now with either of them."

"But aren't you going to go one of them?"

Thyme laughed. "I don't mean you should go to *both* hairdressers. I'll go to the other one at some point, but I have to spend most of the day baking, and we both know you can't do that. Your time's better spent investigating, by pumping a hairdresser for information about Craig and Kayleen."

I threw up my hands in resignation. The first hairdresser I called said she could fit me in. She was probably the better choice of the two hairdressers, because I was stuck on the phone to her for fifteen minutes hearing how her children had been late for school and how she'd already had cancelations that morning.

I told her I wanted a trim. Thyme had pointed out it would be no use having a treatment, because the stylist would leave me alone while the treatment was in my hair.

I headed downtown, dreading the appointment. I'd never had any luck having a simple trim—they always cut off far too much. And as much as I wanted to get information on Craig and Kayleen, I did have to hurry back to mind the shop to leave Thyme free to get on with the baking.

The hairdresser's salon was small and dingy, and I thought I could smell mold as soon as I entered the room. Even the coloring chemicals weren't able to suppress the damp, musty smell. Paint was peeling off the walls, and it had anything but a cheerful atmosphere.

"You must be Amelia," the woman said. "I'm Samantha."

I tried to sum her up. She wasn't overly cheerful, but she wasn't as depressed as her surroundings. "Yes, that's right."

She motioned me to a chair, and at once fastened a cape around my neck. "So, what are we having today?"

"Just a trim, please. I don't want much off it at all."

Samantha clucked her tongue. She selected a strand of my hair, and held it to one side. "But you have *dreadful* split ends," she said in a morbid tone. "They all need to come off."

I clutched the armrests on the chair. "Exactly how much has to come off?" I asked.

Samantha indicated the amount on my hair. "This much," she said firmly.

"No, this much." I held my fingers in the air.

Samantha looked horror-stricken. "You really need it *all* to come off. There's absolutely no point just cutting off *some* of your split ends. You have way too many split ends, and they *all* have to come off. Now, I suggest a good shampoo and conditioner, because your hair is so damaged. You've clearly been using the wrong shampoo and conditioner for your hair. You need to use a good brand. What brand are you using now?"

I shot a quick glance at the brand she was selling, and named it. I knew she was just trying to sell me the brand she had on hand.

Samantha's face fell. "That's a good brand. I don't know why your hair's so damaged." She sighed. "I really need to take all the split ends off."

I had to think fast. "I'll tell you what, I'm a bit scared to have it all off in one go. Why don't you cut off as much as *I* want, and then I'll call some other time and make an appointment for my next day off, once I check the roster."

To my relief, Samantha agreed, albeit reluctantly.

I thought it through. It wasn't going to take her long to cut off the tiny bit of hair I had requested, although I had no doubt she would cut off some more. "I think my hair's damaged because I'm stressed," I said after a moment.

Samantha latched onto the explanation like a Labrador to a tasty treat. "Why are you stressed?" she asked me.

"That man, Scott Plank, was killed in my shop."

Samantha stopped clicking and stared at me in the mirror. "That's right, and Craig and Kayleen were there as well, weren't they?"

I had to choose my words carefully, because I didn't know if they were friends of hers. "That's right." When she didn't respond, but continued snipping away, I decided to risk saying something else. "You know, I'm surprised they weren't arrested, because the three of them were in the shop together, and I only left to go into the back room for a moment."

"They did it," Samantha pronounced angrily.

"They did?" I asked her. "I wouldn't be surprised," I added hastily in an attempt to encourage her to say more.

"It's obvious, isn't it?" She stopped snipping and held her scissors in the air once more.

"Did they have a motive?" I asked hopefully.

"Of course!" Samantha raised her scissors even higher for emphasis. "Scott Plank cheated Kayleen over some land deal. Craig is frightened of her, so that's why he went along with murdering Scott. Craig is a lovely person. He's just really scared of that, that…"

I could see Samantha was having trouble restraining herself from calling Kayleen some fancy words. I was also surprised that she seemed to like Craig.

"Yes, I don't know what Craig is doing with that awful woman," I said. "Do you know Craig well?"

Samantha returned to snipping, a bit more viciously. "Yes, we were dating, but then he dumped me for Kayleen. Of course, he can't be attracted to her, so she must have something over him. That's how I know she's the murderer. I feel so sorry for Craig, but Kayleen would've forced him to do what she wanted. That's just the kind of person she is."

I murmured my sympathies, and then added, "Do you know any details of the land deal that Scott cheated her over? Because if you did, you could tell the police and then they'd know she had a motive."

"No, I don't," Samantha said. "I wish I did. I'd like to see that, that… *woman* end up in prison."

Chapter 14

I didn't think it would be hard to cater the official opening of the new Council Chambers. After all, we were only catering the cakes. There were no meals being served, and we didn't even have to make the coffee, which was just as well, because neither Thyme nor I were trained baristas. I was good at drinking the stuff, but I had no idea how to make it professionally.

Thyme and I had spent the previous day baking. To be more precise, Thyme had spent the previous day baking and I had been her assistant, running around and getting collecting ingredients for her—and no, I hadn't mixed up the salt and the sugar. I hoped so, anyway. I had done all the frosting, and had done a good job, if I do say so myself.

There had been no sign of Fred, or Alder for that matter. I was a little upset. If Alder had meant to kiss me, then why hadn't he contacted since?

I carried a tray of lemon meringue cupcakes from Thyme's car to the back of the new Council Chambers building, in which was their cramped but spotless kitchen. Not a cockroach in sight. That didn't surprise me. Cockroaches could survive a nuclear holocaust, but not a Bayberry Creek winter.

Thyme had tried to teach me to make meringue the previous week, but I'd made rubber instead. Perhaps I should patent it.

"More boring speeches," Thyme said, as she struggled under a huge load of strawberry basil shortcake cupcakes.

"We don't have to be in there listening," I pointed out. "Don't forget, we're setting out the cakes for afterward, so we can stay in here meanwhile."

"And eat as many cupcakes as we like," Thyme said, punctuating her remark by popping a peach cobbler cupcake in her mouth.

I pulled a face. "Thyme, don't eat all the merchandise."

"Go on, you know you want to," she said through a full mouth of crumbs.

I shrugged and devoured a raspberry pavlova cupcake.

"So what's happening with Alder?" she asked me.

I finished eating the cupcake before I spoke. "What do you mean?"

Thyme gave me a playful swat. "You know what I mean! Are you guys dating, or what?"

"I don't really know," I said, choosing my words carefully.

"Well, did he kiss you?"

I felt my cheeks flush, and that was a giveaway. Thyme opened her mouth to say more, but then the hunky constable along with the dour Sergeant Tinsdell walked into the kitchen. I was relieved. I didn't want to get into the whole did-the-entity-make-Alder-kiss-me-or-not scenario, not right now.

The constable stopped and smiled at Thyme, while Sergeant Tinsdell walked straight over to me. "What are you doing here, Miss Spelled?"

I bit back the urge to say 'What does it look like I'm doing?' and instead said, "I'm catering the cupcakes to be served after the opening."

The sergeant simply nodded and walked into the main room, where people were already collected. The constable smiled at Thyme again and then followed him. The two officers took seats at the back of the room.

I turned to Thyme. "So what's happening with you and Constable Gorgeous?"

Thyme stared at a spot on the wall. "I don't know what you're talking about."

I smiled. Now that I had some ammunition, I figured that Thyme wouldn't give me the third degree about Alder to such an extent, not now that I could get my own back.

I busied myself setting out the cupcakes onto nice plates, and onto cupcake tier stands. I had recently bought some vintage and antique bone china stands for occasions such as these. I arranged some cookies and cream cheesecake cupcakes on a Royal Albert china stand that featured a pretty rose design with gold trim and polka dots. Thyme set some triple chocolate cupcakes on a Tuscan china stand, their color set off nicely by the pale mint green of the china. The sugary aroma was hard to resist.

It didn't take long, and soon we had finished. "This is boring," Thyme complained.

"You're telling me," I said. "And I had to shut the shop to be here, so I'm likely losing business."

Thyme rearranged some red velvet cupcakes. "When your business grows, you can employ another staff member."

"That'll be the day," I muttered. "Why are all the speeches so boring? Why can't anyone make an interesting speech? You know, like a speech from a soap opera. That would be funny. I wish they would."

Thyme agreed with me. "This speaker acts like he thinks an election's coming up. He's singing his own praises. It would be comical if it wasn't so boring."

I laughed, and then joined Thyme at the doorway. I could see everyone was restless. I hoped the speakers didn't go overtime, because I wanted to get this over with and head back to the shop. The speaker continued in a monotone, albeit a loud one. "Do you think we could leave, just for a bit?" Thyme asked, but I knew she was joking.

"I'm going to sit down and read a book on my phone," I told her. "Do you have any books downloaded to your phone?"

Thyme's face brightened considerably. "What a good idea!"

Just then everybody gasped. I looked into the main room to see that a new speaker was at the microphone on the stage. Judging by everyone's reactions, this speaker wasn't boring. My stomach sank. I knew at once what was going on.

"Yes, we owe a big thanks to Councilor Robinson for his speech here today. Why do I say this? Well, it was good of him to leave his lunch with his *assistant*, the young and beautiful Miss Austin." Another collective gasp went up from the crowd.

Thyme turned to me. "Did you wish for anything?"

"I must have," I said. "What are we going to do?"

"Well, unless you can figure out how to banish him on the spot, there's nothing we *can* do."

I stood there, frozen to the spot, my hands pressed to my cheeks, as Fred continued his speech.

"I wish you'd stop!" I said. Nothing happened, so I added, "I wish you'd stop speaking right now."

Fred kept speaking, although he looked up at me and smiled. "Why didn't that work?" I said to Thyme.

"How should I know?" she asked me. "Perhaps he has to fulfill your first wish at the expense of later wishes? I have no idea."

"And which Councilor said he was on a business trip to the Sunshine Coast, but there was no business involved. Not if you don't count *funny* business." Fred paused to laugh. "And what about the Councilor who always expands his expenses sheet? I think you'll find those expensive airfares to Sydney are fabricated, considering he drove and didn't fly."

At that point, someone killed the sound to Fred's microphone. Fred waved and walked off the stage.

"I suppose it could've been worse," Thyme said. "Just don't say the W word anymore."

I nodded, too afraid to speak. Just then, I caught sight of the detectives standing at the back of the building. "Look, Thyme, it's the detectives. They must think the murderer's in the room."

"Chances are that the murderer *is*," Thyme said. "I sure hope the detectives are making more progress than we are."

"We're not making any more progress at all," I said.

Thyme nodded solemnly. "Exactly."

The speeches came to an abrupt end after that, so it was lucky that Thyme and I had the cakes already set out nicely. The barista didn't even have the coffee machine warmed up, so everyone headed for the cakes.

I was so busy working that I didn't hear someone speaking to me. I looked up with a start to see Helen Harden. "Amelia, I'm so glad you're not sitting, for once. How's your back?"

"Much better, thanks."

"You should book another appointment.'

I was about to say that I didn't think it necessary, when Thyme caught my eye and nodded her head ever so slightly. "Yes, that's a good idea," I said. "I'll call and make a booking when I'm finished here."

Helen smiled, selected a vanilla cupcake, and turned away to engage in conversation with an elderly lady.

"What was all that about?" I asked Thyme.

"Remember when she said Scott cheated them out of some land, and her husband looked annoyed? Make an appointment and then pump her for information! Not just about her own problems with

Scott, because she probably has more dirt on him than that."

"What a good idea," I said. "I don't know why I didn't think of that sooner."

Chapter 15

Every particle of air in the room was overcome by the pungent smell of oil of wintergreen. I was lying in traction once more, but thankfully, there had been no sign of Fred.

I was even beginning to enjoy myself, although that was probably too strong a statement. I was relaxing, but it did seem a waste of time, considering that my back had felt fine for the last day or so. Still, this was a fact finding mission. I hadn't found too many facts yet, but I was waiting for the right time. Unfortunately, Helen hooked me up to the machine and then left the room. She was speaking to someone on the phone, but I couldn't hear what she was saying, as the door was shut. She did sound quite angry, given that her voice was raised, but I just couldn't make out the words.

As I lay there, I became more and more anxious that I wouldn't find out anything, so I decided to listen in. I carefully unstrapped myself and tiptoed to the door.

"No, I didn't tell the cops!" I heard Helen say. "Anyway, he's dead, so you should be relieved. That takes care of *your* problem, but it doesn't take care of ours."

Unfortunately for me, she then lowered her voice. I pressed my ear to the door, but I couldn't hear any more words, not enough to make sense. Who on earth was she speaking to? I really had to find out.

I was deciding whether to go back and try to strap myself in, when Helen's voice rose again. "Yes, but why don't the cops ask Kayleen? Scott sold her a block of land. He told her the sewer system was available and close, but he lied. It turned out that the sewer was a long way away. That meant that she couldn't build a house on it, not unless she put in a very expensive sewer pump station. The cost was prohibitive, so she was stuck with the block. She couldn't even sell it, not for anywhere near the price she paid for it. Now that block's just a millstone around her neck." She paused for a moment before continuing. "Yes, Kayleen's a mean piece of work. I wouldn't put it past her to murder someone, not at all. If you ask me, she's the one who killed him!"

There was silence for a while. I started to move back to the table, when Helen spoke again. "No one knows he was blackmailing you. No, I won't tell the cops. You don't need to worry. Truly."

I wasn't game to push my luck, so I hurried back to the table. Just as well I did, as Helen came in the room while I was attaching the buckles to my ankles.

"Amelia, what are you doing?"

"I thought you must've left, so I was going to look for you."

Helen smiled. "No, remember I said it would take fifteen minutes? You have another five."

I laid down and she closed the straps. I had to think fast. Who had she been speaking to on the phone? Someone was blackmailing the victim and didn't want the police to know. It wasn't Kayleen, because Helen had mentioned Kayleen, but Kayleen herself did have a motive for murder. Still, I had to find out who Scott was blackmailing. Could it have been his ex-wife, Penny? She was in town at the time of the murder. I spoke as Helen was adjusting the traction machine. "I didn't see Penny Plank at the memorial service, although I did see her in town the other day."

Helen nodded. "There was no love lost between Penny and Scott. She'd hardly go to the memorial service for him. I'm sure she won't even go to his funeral."

"Oh," I said, trying to inject surprise into my voice. "I assumed Penny was only in town for the service." Helen shook her head, but didn't say anything, so I continued. "Do they have any children?" So as not to appear to be too nosy, I added, "It would be awful if they did."

Helen made her way to the door. As her hand reached the door knob, she turned to me. "Yes, she has three children."

"How awful," I said, "losing their dad."

Helen frowned. "They haven't seen him for years. The divorce was very nasty, and he did everything he could to avoid giving Helen child support. She really hated him."

Helen left, leaving me once more alone with my thoughts. Was Scott blackmailing his ex-wife? Even if he wasn't, she appeared to have had a nasty relationship with him. Yet was that enough reason to give her a motive for murder? And why had she been in town at the very time her husband was murdered?

And, if it wasn't Penny, who was the person on the other end of the phone? Scott had been blackmailing whoever it was. And Kayleen was even more so looking like a probable suspect.

I now had more questions than answers.

Chapter 16

After work, Thyme and I headed straight to Ruprecht's shop, *Glinda's*. I had received a brief text from Alder saying he was out of town, and would be in touch as soon as he got back. I supposed that was better than nothing.

Camino was already there, as was Mint. Camino, thankfully, was for once dressed in her street clothes. "We're exhausted," Mint said with a sigh. "We've been reading through translations of ancient texts to try to find a way to banish Fred."

Ruprecht shook his finger at her. "Now Mint, I told you it would be no use. Amelia's the only one who can banish that spirit."

I yawned and stretched. I wasn't in a spirit-banishing mood. The last few days had left me tired.

"How about a nice cup of hot lavender tea?" Ruprecht asked me.

"Thanks, but I think I'm calm enough already," I replied. "I don't suppose there's any wine on offer?"

Mint held up her own wine glass. "Sure is! Red or white?"

"White would be great, thanks."

Soon we were all sitting around Ruprecht's table. That's how Ruprecht preferred it when we held meetings such as this one.

The light was dim, being provided only by the candles that perched in the sockets of the sconces, as well as three black verbena-scented candles in the center of the table. *Glinda's* always held a suggestion of the otherworldly. Who knew what shades dwelled in the recesses of its recesses and alcoves? Glinda's was entirely enigmatic, and that was one of the reasons I loved the store.

I drew my attention back to the matter at hand. "I've been meaning to ask you, Ruprecht, how has the spirit managed to get into my house, yet hasn't been in yours? I assume you have your house spelled somehow to keep it out?"

"That's right, Amelia. I have protection spells and wards all over my house."

"I would've thought my house had those. I suppose I need to put some up?"

The others laughed. "No Amelia," Ruprecht said. "Your house *itself* is a ward, one big ward. If that spirit meant you any harm, it wouldn't have been able to get into the house."

"But surely the spirit isn't well meaning toward me?" I said in disbelief.

"Not everything is black and white," Ruprecht said. "Haints themselves have different personalities.

This appears to be a mischievous haint. Has it taken your keys or perhaps your purse?"

"What do you mean?"

"Have your keys been misplaced lately, and then you've looked for them, only to find them appear somewhere that you had already looked?"

I frowned. "No, that hasn't happened."

Ruprecht appeared to be thinking that over for a few moments. "Okay, well then, I still think it's a trickster type of spirit, but it least it isn't doing anything like that. That's something to be grateful for, I suppose."

"Have we ruled out Fred as a murderer then?" I said hopefully.

Ruprecht shook his head. "I'm afraid not, Amelia. It does appear to be a haint with some sort of a sense of humor, but a haint's sense of humor is not that of a human's. I suggest you figure out how to come into your powers, and banish him, as soon as you are able."

I was frustrated. "But how? You've said that before. How do I find a way to come into my powers?"

Ruprecht looked solemn. "Only you can find that answer, Amelia. For that, you need to look deep inside yourself."

I nodded, although I didn't have a clue what he was talking about. I just hoped he wouldn't go on to quote Confucius, Socrates, or Master Yoda.

"Amelia found out something interesting today," Thyme informed them.

I shot her a grateful look for changing the subject. "Yes, I went to Helen Harden, the physical therapist, for another back treatment, but really to try to get information. As you know, at the memorial service she said that Scott had cheated her over a land deal."

"So you found out about that, did you?" Camino said.

"No I didn't, so we still need to find out about that," I said. "But I overheard her talking to someone on the phone. She seemed quite annoyed about something, and she promised the person that she wouldn't tell the cops that Scott was blackmailing whoever it was."

Ruprecht leaned forward, the candlelight flickering over the sharp angles of his face. "Did she mention a name?"

"No, that's just it. She didn't. But she did mention Kayleen's name, so obviously she wasn't speaking to Kayleen. She did mention that Scott sold Kayleen a piece of worthless land. Apparently, he told her the sewer service was available, but he lied. Now Kayleen's stuck with the property."

"We need to look into that more," Ruprecht said. "We now know that he swindled Kayleen, and also cheated Helen and her husband Henry over some land. We need to find out the specific details, because that is likely to have some bearing on the murder."

"Who would know about it?" Thyme asked.

I shrugged. "It's a wonder the whole town doesn't know."

"It shouldn't be too hard to get the information," Ruprecht said. "Now let's look at the facts before us. Scott Plank had crooked dealings with Kayleen, and with Henry and Helen Harden. He was also blackmailing someone else."

"And there's more," I said. "Helen told me that Penny Plank despised her ex-husband. She said that Penny would never have gone to his memorial service, and she doubted Penny would even go to the funeral. She didn't tell me why Penny was in town the day of Scott's murder—I mean, I don't think she knew. The only other piece of information I got out of her was that Scott did everything he could to avoid paying child support to Penny."

One of the candles on the table had burned all the way down, so Ruprecht replaced it with another large black candle, and lighted it. He sat back down and stared at the flame for a while. "So that gives us five suspect groups," he said finally. "And in no particular order, they are Fred, Penny Plank, Helen and Henry Harden, Craig and Kayleen, and the mysterious blackmailer."

"Where do we go from here?" I asked him. As soon as the words were out of my mouth, I at once feared he would tell me one again to come into my own and banish the haint, while quoting ancient philosophers in a dead foreign language, so I hurried to add, "I think we need to find out what Penny Plank was doing in town at the time."

"Quite right," Ruprecht said, and to my relief, he didn't say anything more.

"And we need to find out who the blackmailer was," Camino said, "but I have no idea how we're going to do that."

Ruprecht cleared his throat. "Something we *can* do is find out about Scott's crooked land deals. I'm quite sure that if he cheated Kayleen as well as Helen and Henry Harden, then he would have done the same to others as well."

"But that could give us more than five suspects," I said sadly.

"Maybe so," Ruprecht said, "but it could also help us narrow down the suspects. Tomorrow is Saturday, so Amelia, why don't you and Thyme drive to Port Macquarie to see what you can find out about Penny Plank? Perhaps she's having an affair with someone from Bayberry Creek."

"Do you think so?" I asked, interested.

Ruprecht smiled. "No, I don't especially think so. It was just an example of the information you could find out about her."

"But the drive to Port Macquarie is ghastly, right down that horrible mountain," Thyme said. "I always get carsick."

"How long does it take to get there?" I asked.

"It's a few hours," Thyme said. "We can't leave there after we shut the shop at midday and go down and back in the same day. It would be tiring—we'd be back too late at night, and besides, it wouldn't give us much daylight to spy on her."

"Mint can mind the shop for you."

Mint shot a look at her grandfather, but then nodded. "I don't mind. That's a good division of labor. The two of you go to Port Macquarie to spy on Penny, while Ruprecht and Camino can ask questions. I'll mind the shop."

Thyme did not look impressed. "It's a horrible drive. Port isn't all that far from here, it's just that you can't drive fast when you're spending most of that time going up and down the mountain road. A really winding road."

"Doesn't sound very appealing, but we could find out some really good information. Plus we can easily drive there and back in the one day." I gave Thyme a reassuring smile, but she didn't smile back.

"And Camino and I will ask around about Scott's real estate dealings," Ruprecht said.

Chapter 17

"I can't believe they didn't have any coffee shops open in that town we just went through," I grumbled.

"You've said that about five times, Amelia." Thyme clutched her stomach. "They probably don't open until nine, and we went through town well before that. Just as well I didn't have anything in my stomach, though, or I'd be sick."

I shot a worried look at Thyme. She wasn't exaggerating about being prone to carsickness. We had only just hit the winding roads and already her face was a ghastly shade of green. "Just tell me if you want me to pull over," I said. "Try to give me some warning, because it doesn't look like there are many opportunities to pull off the road."

Thyme merely grunted, and stuck her head out the window.

I swerved to miss a bush turkey. It was considerably past dawn, so I was fairly certain that kangaroos wouldn't be jumping out in front of the car, but I tried to keep my eye on both sides of the road just in case, not that it would do any good. Kangaroos move like lightning.

"You were right, Thyme, this isn't a very nice road."

"It's like this for miles," Thyme managed to say. "This is nothing. This is just the beginning—it gets worse after Gingers Creek. At any rate, living up at Bayberry Creek, whenever you want to get to the coast you've gotta go down a big mountain whichever route you take. This is nowhere near as bad as the Dorrigo mountain."

I made a mental note to avoid the Dorrigo mountain. Still, as far as mountains went, this one wasn't horrendous. There were no scary cliff faces at the edge of the road, at least not that I could see. If any existed, they were obscured by the towering eucalyptus trees and thick undergrowth. It was just that the winding road was unrelenting, and slow going at that.

I drove on for another thirty minutes in silence. There wasn't a word from Thyme until we reached a big sign heralding the approach of the only café on the mountain. "Look," she said with obvious relief. "We can pull over there. I can walk around to get some fresh air if you want to use the bathroom."

I pulled off the road, in front of the store that looked something like a giant log cabin, an oasis in a vast stretch of rainforest. There was plenty of parking, and about five cars already parked there.

Thyme struggled out of the car and then slumped over the hood, while I headed for the big sign that said 'Ladies.'"

I paused with my hand on the door, wondering why the ladies' bathroom was right next to the alfresco dining area. I opened the door and walked in, and then saw to my dismay at a there was a giant window directly overlooking the alfresco dining area. Sure, the window was frosted, but it wasn't quite frosted enough, if you ask me.

The color had returned to Thyme's face, and she was pacing up and down next to the car. "You're looking a lot better," I said.

"You're back fast," she said by way of response.

"Are there any other public bathrooms around here?" I asked her. "That one has a huge window. I'm sure anyone eating out there could look straight in!"

Thyme chuckled. "Why did you think I didn't go in there?"

"Please tell me there's another one close. I'm going to have to go back if there isn't."

"Yes, the composting toilets are just down the hill." Thyme pointed over her shoulder to the left.

"That's a relief!"

Thyme sniggered. "You mightn't say that when you see them."

I motioned for her to get back in the car in a hurry. I'd had two cups of coffee before I collected Thyme that morning, and they were beginning to take their toll. At the bottom of the hill was a huge parking area and a green corrugated iron building. "You go first, given that you're so desperate," Thyme said.

I didn't need to be told twice. I hurried up the ramp to the composting toilets.

Several minutes later, I was back at the car. "Why didn't you warn me about the smell of the composting toilets?" I asked Thyme.

She shrugged. "It's either a ghastly smell, or you have an audience. Which do you prefer?"

I had to admit that she had a point. Soon we were back on our way, winding down the mountain on our way to Wauchope.

It seemed like an age before we were down the mountain, and it probably was, given that I had to pull over for Thyme about three times on the way, giving her the opportunity to walk up and down to get some fresh air.

Mercifully, once down the mountain, the road was fast and flat. "I'm beginning to feel hungry now," Thyme said.

I pointed to a sign. "Wauchope's just under an hour away."

Thyme groaned. "I need to eat before that. Can you stop at Long Flat shop?"

"What do you mean? There's a long flat shop?"

Thyme laughed. "No silly, that's the name of the town. Long Flat."

We bought food at Long Flat and took off all our outer layers. It was so much warmer here than in Bayberry Creek, and it wasn't all that far away as the crow flies.

"Remind me again why we're living in Bayberry Creek and not here," I said to Thyme when we finally reached the outskirts of Port Macquarie.

"You say that now, but wait until we reach the beaches," Thymes said. "Then you'll be *really* sorry we don't live here. I think there are nine beaches here. We'll have to come down for the weekend one time."

My mind went straight to Alder. This would be a great romantic getaway. Of course, thinking about Alder brought up the unpleasant thoughts that had been bugging me ever since he kissed me. Had he only kissed me because I wished he would?

Thyme was punching an address into the GPS. "I only know my way to Port Macquarie, so this will get us to Penny Plank's address."

"What are we going to do when we get there?" We had planned to discuss that matter on the way down, but Thyme had been too sick for any conversation.

"Play it by ear," Thyme said nonchalantly.

"Quick, stop the car!" Thyme said as I turned into Penny Plank's street.

I did as she asked. "Why?"

"Look, that's her house over there."

Penny's house was a few houses away from where I had parked. She was trying to get five children and a medium sized dog into her car. "That's a lot of kids," I said. "I don't know how she manages."

"Especially if Scott wasn't paying child support," Thyme said. "But how lucky are we! We can just follow her."

I shook my head. "I still don't know what Ruprecht expects us to find."

I turned the car around, and followed her at a distance, until she came to a busy road. I kept a couple of cars between us, and stayed behind her for over five minutes. She finally turned left at a sign that said, 'Nobbys Beach,' so I pulled in behind her.

I could see the beach directly at the side of my car, and there was a cliff edge. I was on the outside edge of the road with the sheer drop right next to the car, and I don't like heights at the best of times. I broke into a cold sweat. To my horror, a huge Jeep Grand Cherokee headed up the hill straight for us. "There's not enough room for us to pass each other," I said in a panic.

"Just keep going, you'll be all right," Thyme said weakly.

I froze. I stopped the car and just sat there, until the man driving the other car edged past me slowly. I then continued down the short distance to the parking area, relieved that on the way back up the hill, I would not be on the cliff side.

Penny had parked on the left side of the parking area and was getting the children and the dog out of the car. I parked on the opposite side of the parking area, and to my horror, there was another sheer cliff drop. This one was directly in front of me. There was no guardrail and only some tiny wooden stumps between me and a precipitous plunge to a certain death.

"Amelia, can you make really sure that the car's in reverse when we leave?" Thyme asked, her voice fraught with anxiety.

"You can be sure I will," I said nervously. I wiped my sweaty palms on my jeans and tried to steady my breathing.

We waited until Penny was out of sight, and then we walked over to the beach, pausing at the top of the long flight of wooden steps down to the beach itself.

"Look, here's a sign that says 'Dogs only,'" Thyme said. "We don't have a dog."

"It's not as if anyone's going to arrest us for not having a dog," I pointed out. "What will we do? Will we wait in the car until she comes back, or go down to the beach?"

"We'll be way too conspicuous going down to the beach without a dog," Thyme said.

I was sure she was right. Everyone on the beach, as far as I could see, had at least one dog. "We could wait to see if she's meeting anyone, I suppose."

Thyme clutched my arm. "I have an idea! Quick! Let's drive back to her house."

"And do what?"

"We can question her neighbors about her, pretend we're visiting or something and looking for her."

I tapped my chin. "I suppose so. But what if someone describes us to her later?"

"She's never met us," Thyme said. "Hurry, we don't know how long she's going to spend at the beach, but her being here gives us some time to question neighbors."

On the short distance to the car, at least five people stopped to ask us if we'd lost our dog. We said that we had just met a friend with a dog.

After commenting on how friendly the locals were, I gingerly reversed the car, and then drove back up the steep hill. This time, I didn't pass another car, but I wasn't too worried about doing so, given that I wasn't on the cliff edge this time. The GPS led us straight back to Penny's house without incident.

"Follow my lead," Thyme said.

I nodded, wishing I had her confidence. My heart was racing and my palms were sweaty. Thyme walked to Penny's door and knocked on it, and then made a show of looking around. I noticed a woman peering at us over the fence, so I nudged Thyme.

Thyme waved to the lady and then walked over to her. "Hi, we're friends of Penny's from out of town. We haven't seen her in ages, but she knew we were passing through town today and she's expecting us. I thought she'd be back by now. She did say she was taking the kids and the dog to the beach first though, so I suppose she just got held up."

The lady nodded. "Yeah, she only left a short time ago. Perhaps she got the time wrong. Those kids are a handful, and so's the dog."

"It must be hard for the children with their father dying recently," Thyme said.

The woman snorted rudely. "Those kids didn't even know they *had* a father. He's never paid child-support and he's never even been here to see them."

"I'm surprised he's managed to avoid paying child support," I said, "especially since he has a legal obligation to do so."

"But that's what happens when you have expensive lawyers," the woman said. "Penny often says that he's probably paid the lawyers more than he would've ended up paying in child support, but he's just so spiteful."

"I'm not surprised that Penny won't be going to his funeral," Thyme said.

"She's probably just happy that someone did the job for her," the lady said.

Thyme and I exchanged glances. "What do you mean?" Thyme asked her.

"Well, there was that time when she tried to hit Scott with her car, and he ended up in the hospital."

"But that wasn't recently," I said. I guessed it wasn't by the way she mentioned it, but I wanted her to think that I knew all about it, especially if she was going to tell us that Penny had actually tried to murder her husband. It seemed to pay off.

"I'd forgotten about that," Thyme lied. "Was she charged for it?"

The woman laughed. "No, she wasn't even charged. It was when Scott came here to yell at her and tell her she'd never get any child support out of him, and she was just on her way out when he arrived. She reversed over him, and broke his leg in three places. You know, she never had any luck with the law over getting child-support, because he keeps delaying it, but Lady Luck was sure on her side that day."

She paused for breath, and Thyme and I remained silent. Fortunately, she continued. "Scott called the police, of course, but Penny pretended to be upset. She said that he'd yelled at her and threatened to take the kids away from her, and as she was on her way to collect them from school, she became distraught and didn't realize he was standing directly behind her car."

"That was lucky for her," I said. "It seems a rather lame excuse. I'm so glad they believed Penny, though," I added quickly.

"As you know, Penny's a drama teacher, so she's quite a good actress. She had those cops wrapped around her little finger. She was really pleased with herself. She was only sorry she missed him, and only hit his leg." The woman narrowed her eyes.

Thyme pointedly looked at her watch, and I took the hint. "Oh, I just forgot that we haven't brought the children any gifts," I said to Thyme. "You know how upset they get when we don't bring gifts for them."

The lady appeared to believe me—after all, why wouldn't she? "You probably passed a big shopping mall on your way here," she said helpfully. "Settlement City. I'm sure you'll have time to go there and buy gifts and get back about the time Penny and the kids get home."

We both thanked her, and beat a hasty retreat.

"Jackpot!" Thyme exclaimed as soon as we were out of earshot. "Let's go to the nearest café and google any old news story about it."

I unlocked the car and jumped in. "There probably isn't anything about it," I said once Thyme was in the car, too, "given that she wasn't even charged."

Thyme fastened her seatbelt. "Well, we can eat, surely? I'm starved. It won't hurt to google while we're stuffing our faces. We can kill two birds with one stone."

We soon found a cafe on the Hastings River. To our delight, there were tables right by the water.

"We can relax and have a good lunch," Thyme said. "Penny already tried to kill Scott once. You know what that means?"

"No," I said. I was busy looking at the menu. "Look, they have organic wine. I can't have any because I'm driving," I said as a hint.

"Sorry, Amelia, but I can't drive back. I know they say people only get carsick if they're passengers, but I actually get really bad if I'm driving. I'd drive if I could, but I can't, not around winding roads. Anyway, my treat for lunch, to make up for you driving all the way."

I thanked her, and then added, "Anyway, what were you going to say?"

"I was going to say that the detectives would have no idea that she already tried to kill Scott once. We'll have to tell them."

"But we know that there's no evidence against her, because she wasn't charged," I said, running my finger down on the menu, "as much as I'd like the murderer to be Penny and not Fred."

Thyme was unperturbed. "That doesn't matter. They can question her nosy neighbor. Besides, surely it's on record that Scott called the police, even if they didn't take any action. There would have to be a police report. Anyway, what are you having to eat? And your usual coffee?"

Thyme went to pay, while I looked at my iPad. As I expected, I couldn't find a thing about Penny trying to run over Scott. I couldn't find much on the woman at all. She had a Facebook account, but no Instagram or Snapchat, not even Twitter. The privacy settings on her Facebook account were high, so that was no help, either.

I told Thyme as soon as she returned to the table. "No matter," she said. "At least we have something to tell the police. You know, the people in Port Macquarie are all super nice. It must be the sea air. They're all so happy. Weird, isn't it!" Before I could reply, she added, "Well, I'm sure it's her. She's the murderer. Penny killed her ex-husband."

Chapter 18

It was a long drive home. Thyme wasn't as sick on the return journey, so we made good time, and arrived well before the Bayberry Creek Police Station closed for the day. We had worked on our cover story on the way.

The detectives were out, but Sergeant Tinsdell and Constable Dawson said they'd pass on a message. Thyme launched straight into her story. "Amelia and I took the day off and went to Port Macquarie. We happened to run into a neighbor of Penny Plank's, and she told us that Penny hit Scott with her car last year."

"That's right," I said. "The neighbor said that Scott called the police, but Penny wasn't charged. She broke his leg in three places. There has to be a police report on file."

Sergeant Tinsdell did not seem at all pleased to receive the information, although Constable Dawson, on the other hand, seemed mighty pleased to see Thyme. "Port Macquarie's a lovely place," Dawson said to Thyme, ignoring me. I might as well not have been there. "I was stationed there for a year. I'd love to go back again soon."

Tinsdell cleared his throat loudly, and Dawson shuffled uncomfortably. "I hope you two weren't snooping into police matters," Tinsdell barked. "I didn't know you girls knew Mrs. Plank."

"We don't," Thyme said. "Well, we have to leave now that we've given you the information. We have a baking deadline."

We hurried out of the police station and got in the car. I cast a furtive glance over my shoulder. "You were right, Thyme! I really didn't think that would work. I expected Tinsdell would call us back."

Thyme giggled. "How about I go and fill Ruprecht and the others in on what's happened? You should go straight home to bed. After all, you were the one doing all the driving. Don't forget, Camino's yard sale is tomorrow, and she wants us all to help out."

I groaned. "I *will* go straight to bed. I'm so tired I can barely keep my eyes open."

"And don't open the door to Penny Plank. I mean it! Murderers always seem to end up at your house."

"I won't." Thyme narrowed her eyes, so I added, "Seriously! I won't."

I was ravenous, but I was too tired to go and wait in line for take-out. My back was sore again for the first time in a few days, no doubt from all the driving. I wanted to do nothing more than take a long hot bath, lie on the couch, and stare at the ceiling.

I opened the door to the sound of battle. It was no surprise—the house was still watching the *Game of Thrones* marathon. Just what I didn't need, more war scenes. I was in the mood for a good romantic comedy.

After I fed Willow and Hawthorn who made it abundantly clear they wouldn't leave me alone until I fed them, I ran a bath. On Saturday nights I was in the habit of having a jinx-breaking bath, one into which I'd poured sea salt, Epsom salts, and uncrossing herbs such as rue, hyssop, and lemongrass. I normally bathed between two candles and then air dried myself, but tonight I just didn't have the energy. I just threw in a handful of sea salt and a handful of agrimony and hoped for the best.

I was relaxed, lying with my eyes closed, when I had the feeling I was being watched. I opened my eyes to see Hawthorn and Willow sitting on the edge of the bath, staring at me. It was rather unnerving, to say the least. "Shoo!" I said, but that, of course, had no effect. They were cats, after all, so they weren't going to do anything I wanted them to do.

The long hot bath refreshed me. I know that sounds counter-intuitive, but it did. I went into my bedroom to put on my pajamas, but decided to look through my closet to find items to donate to the yard sale. After all, it was for charity. I threw a few things on the pile, and then spied my old cocktail dress. It was black, clingy, and oh-so-tight. I loved that dress, but I had no idea if it still fitted. Oh well, there was one way to find out. If it didn't, I'd give it to Camino to sell.

The dress went over my shoulders okay, but that's when things got difficult. I managed, after a bit of struggle, to pull it over my hips. I reached for the zip, which didn't want to move freely at all. I tugged and tugged at it, but it got stuck half-way. I turned my back to the mirror to see how to free it, and that's when I screamed.

I had back cleavage.

The cats ran in to see what the emergency was. "I have back cleavage," I informed them, but they didn't care. "How did it happen?" I asked my reflection. It certainly wasn't from my own cooking. Perhaps I'd been eating too many cupcakes. Or perhaps the dress had shrunk. That was more a cheerful thought.

I tried to get it off, but the zip wouldn't budge. I went into the kitchen to get scissors. I'd have to cut it off. While I was looking for the scissors, there was a knock on the door. My heart beat out of my chest. Was it Penny Plank, here to kill me? The house had let her knock, but perhaps the house wanted us to play Arya Stark versus the Waif.

I ran back into my room and grabbed my phone. If it was Penny, then I'd call the police rather than letting her in. I crept to the front door. "Hello?" I said nervously.

"Hello, it's me," said a man's voice.

"Alder?" I opened the door.

He stared at my dress. "Are you on your way out?'

"No."

"Do you have guests?'

I shook my head. "No."

Alder frowned. "Are you expecting anyone?"

"No," I said once more.

"You're wearing an evening dress."

"Yes." I figured I should explain why I was in the dress, but I didn't know where to start. "Please come in." I backed away so he wouldn't see my back cleavage. I backed all the way into the living room. "Please sit down." I was pleased that the house had turned off the TV.

"I've brought you take-out and a bottle of wine. I don't have time to stay and eat, but I won't refuse a small glass of wine, and then I'll leave you alone to rest. I know you must be tired after that long drive up and down the mountain."

I felt like a started wombat caught in the headlights. "How, how did you know?" I stuttered.

Alder placed the bottle of wine and the take-out on the table, and sat on the couch. "Penny called me and told me that two women were asking questions about her."

I felt silly for not even considering that. "You didn't tell her it was us?"

"No. Anyway, she assumed it was a couple of detectives."

I sat down. There was a loud ripping sound. At least the zip had worked its way free, to look on the bright side. "That was my dress," I said stupidly.

Alder nodded. I thought his mouth twitched, but I wasn't sure.

"Camino has a yard sale tomorrow, so I was trying on my old clothes to see if they still fitted."

Alder nodded again.

"Um, I'll just go and change," I said. I stood up and backed out of the room. Once I was in the hall and out of sight, I turned and hurried to my room. I ripped off the damaged dress and replaced it with jeans and a crossover jersey top. At least now I could breathe deeply. "What is *he* doing here?" I whispered to Hawthorn who was sprawled on my bed. "Not that I'm complaining!"

I went to the kitchen to fetch wine glasses before returning to the dining room.

Alder spoke first. "Penny is my client. I know she didn't do it."

"She seems the obvious suspect," I said, while Alder poured the wine.

"I'm sure Penny isn't sorry in the least that Scott's dead," Alder said, "but if she was going to kill him, she would've done it years ago. Besides, you've seen her. She's slender. She wouldn't have the strength to strangle Scott."

I sipped the wine before speaking. "Maybe she hired a hitman."

Alder smiled. "If she hired a hitman, then she would've made sure she had an alibi. More to the point, she wouldn't have been in town the day Scott was murdered."

Well, duh! That was obvious, I thought. *I didn't think that one through*. Aloud I said, "Do the police think it's her?"

Alder shook his head. "No, they don't. Have you seen the haint lately?"

My stomach clenched. "Why, do you think the haint murdered Scott?"

"I don't think it was the haint," Alder said carefully. "I think it was a human, a man, but I don't know why he chose your store to murder Scott. Penny was in town that day. She had an appointment with me. She wanted me to find out anything I could, any dirt on Scott, because he'd applied to the court for access to see the children. He hadn't wanted to see them for years."

I narrowed my eyes. "The timing does make her seem suspect, you must admit."

Alder shrugged. "Like I said, she'd have made sure she was out of town if she'd arranged to have him murdered." He downed his wine and then stood up.

I stood up, too.

"Amelia, I don't know how to tell you this, so I'll come straight out and say it. You're in danger. I did a divination."

I was struck speechless. "Me?" I managed to say.

Alder took both my hands in his. "Amelia, promise me you'll be careful."

And then, with a swish of his long black coat, he was gone.

I stared after him, wondering why he hadn't kissed me this time. Had he only kissed me at his apartment because Fred had made him? I was now even more certain that this was the case.

Chapter 19

I woke up and stretched. As soon as Willow and Hawthorn saw my eyes open, both walked up the bed and peered at me, and commenced their cacophony of loud meowing. This was our regular morning routine. It would be nice to have some time in bed to wake up properly, but I don't think anyone who had a cat would have that luxury.

I reluctantly climbed out of bed, put on my fake Ugg boots that I'd bought on sale at Payless, and then staggered to the kitchen.

I filled two bowls, and the cats ate as if they were starving. I noted that their bowl of dry food was half full, so I put a little more in it. Willow stopped eating his food and dived on the dry food. "There was already plenty in there," I informed him. "This is a Sunday, and humans like to sleep in on a Sunday morning."

The cats kept eating as if I had said nothing of interest.

As I switched on the coffee machine, I lamented the fact that I'd had no time to come into my own as a Dark Witch, whatever that expression meant. I had intended to try to figure it out, but life kept getting in the way.

I took my coffee and went into the living room, where I stretched out on the couch, grateful that the house wasn't watching *Game of Thrones* at this time of day. I suppose even the house liked to sleep on a Sunday morning.

I half intended to fall back to sleep, when I remembered what day it was. Camino's yard sale. My Dark Witchy self would have to wait. I groaned and then downed the rest of my coffee in one gulp.

When I arrived at Camino's, caffeine-fueled and clutching my clothing donations, I saw a big sign adorning the lawn: *All money going to charity - The Parachute Widows*. I winced at the thought of all those poor men falling to their death. Sure, I have an active imagination, but the image was just too gruesome. I knew that parachuting wasn't a safe sport, of course, but I had no idea that sufficient men were killed doing it to warrant a charity for their widows.

Camino was already serving customers, so I arranged my clothes donations as best I could. I was pleased to see Thyme arrive. I'd told her she could park at my house to leave room for the yard sale customers to park outside Camino's house. "Ruprecht agrees that Penny's the killer," Thyme said by way of greeting, and then yawned loudly.

I yawned, too. "I don't think she is. Alder told me why she was in town that day. She's a client of his, and he said she definitely didn't do it."

Thyme raised her eyebrows and stared at me. "What? When did he tell you that?"

"He came over last night."

Thyme's eyebrows rose even higher. "He did? Did you…"

I interrupted her. "Of course not! I hardly know him."

"Not as well as you'd like to." Thyme winked at me.

I playfully swatted her with the leg of my old jeans. I didn't mind being teased—after all, that was far better than her having an attitude to Alder. She certainly seemed to be warming to him. And he had been quite warm to me, but had he only kissed me because I'd wished he would? I just had to get some more time to figure out this whole thing.

"Ruprecht is still looking into other suspects, though."

I nodded. I was pleased about that. It would make things really awkward if Ruprecht and the others insisted that Penny was the killer, when Alder insisted that she wasn't.

Camino hurried over to us. "Would you two serve the drinks and food?"

We both said that we would. In fact, we'd already agreed to do so, which is why I'd donated several trays of cupcakes. "Thyme and I will go fetch the cupcakes," I told her. Camino thanked me profusely. "I always like to help out a charity," I said. "I had no idea that parachuting is responsible for so many deaths."

Camino looked blank. "What do you mean?"

It was my turn to be confused. "I mean your charity, of course, *The Parachute Widows*, the wives of men who died parachuting," I added to spell it out.

Camino's jaw dropped. "Oh Amelia, you're just too funny," she said with a chuckle. "It's not for that! No, it's for women whose husbands are too obsessed with parachuting. You know, like football widows." Camino chuckled again.

I looked at Thyme, but she shrugged.

Camino kept talking. "I've assigned you and Thyme the job of making non-alcoholic cocktails with little umbrellas in them, since you'll be doing the food anyway. Umbrellas are the closest things to parachutes. Oh, look, another customer!" Camino rubbed her hands together with glee and hurried away.

I turned to Thyme. "I'm shocked that it could be a registered charity. Was Camino joking?"

Thyme shook her head. "Sadly, I don't think she is. I'm not saying she's right, though. Maybe she's confused."

I didn't know whether or not I hoped she *was* confused. I didn't want lots of men to die parachuting, but the alternative was surely not charity-worthy. I shrugged and gestured to the trestle table. "Oh well, let's get set up."

We hadn't finished setting up before the first customers arrived. Both of us had to serve, and we still hadn't made the non-alcoholic cocktails. At the first break in customers, Thyme gathered the ingredients. "Amelia, I should make them and you can put the umbrellas in."

I agreed it was a safer option. I was sure I was better at making drinks than baking, but it was best not to take the risk. We worked together and soon had an array of dazzling cocktails, all strangely in plastic cups and adorned by multi-colored umbrellas. We finished just in time, because about ten cars arrived at once.

As the crowd walked onto Camino's lawn, it seemed they all spied the cupcakes and cocktails at once. The people as one group headed straight for us.

Just as I readied myself to serve them, the umbrellas left the cocktails and rose into the air. Everyone gasped. The umbrellas hovered for a moment around head height, and then rose even higher. I hadn't even felt a breeze, let alone a strong wind.

Thyme clutched my arm. "What's happening?"

I had no clue, but then I noticed a man standing in front of me, smiling at me. He was wearing one of those novelty spinning bow ties. "Fred!" I exclaimed.

"Make him stop," Thyme said urgently.

"Fred, stop!" I said. "Fred, I wish you'd stop."

My words had no effect, and Fred continued to smile at me as the umbrellas rose ever higher. Without warning, they all floated to the ground in unison, and broke apart upon contact.

"I get it," a teenager said. "Cool! They were meant to be parachutes, weren't they? Very clever. How did you do that?"

"Magnets," I said, hoping the guy wasn't a physics student and would press me for details. Luckily, people simply stepped up to the table to buy cocktails that were now minus their umbrellas.

"I'm sure I didn't say the W word this time!" I hissed at Thyme.

Thyme agreed. "I'm certain you didn't. This means he's getting worse. This is pretty bad, Amelia."

"I know," I said grimly.

"Do something! I'll look after the customers."

I walked away from the crowd, over to my fence, against the tall eucalyptus tree on the border of my land and Camino's. I was hoping Fred would follow me so I could talk to him, but he mingled with the crowd.

This was it—I couldn't put it off any longer. Everyone had told me that now was the time to be coming to my powers, so I would have to make it a priority. Matters were escalating, and who knows what Fred would do next.

I was by myself. I had no candles, crystals, or herbs. I didn't have my wand. I just had myself. All I could do was summon the magic within me.

I stood still and closed my eyes, and tried to feel the pulse of the earth running through me. First I felt nothing, then I felt a little spark, a hint of something. I didn't know what it was, but I didn't focus on that. Instead, I let it build. As I felt the power rising within me, I focused on Fred stopping what he was doing, and going away.

I could say a surge of power pulsed through me, but it wasn't quite that. It was as if I had settled into something. I opened my eyes, and Fred had vanished.

Thyme hurried over to me. "He just went, like that!" She snapped her fingers.

"Did anyone else see?"

Thyme shook her head. "I don't think so. He was at the back of the crowd."

I breathed a huge sigh of relief.

"How did you do it?"

"You know how you want a parking place somewhere where it's unlikely that you'd get one, and you hold it with your mind just so, and then you get it?"

Thyme stared at me. "You can do that?"

"Yes, can't everyone?"

"No! How long have you been able to do that?"

"For as long as I can remember." I didn't know why she was so shocked. "Anyway, it was the same feeling as that. I held it with my mind just so—it's hard to explain—and the umbrellas stopped, and then Fred vanished."

"Has he gone for good?"

I shook my head. "No. Don't ask me how I know, but he hasn't." That was next on my To Do list.

Chapter 20

I was tired, exhausted in fact. Recent events had taken their toll, not only the murder, but I was in two minds about my relationship with Alder. Sure, I wanted a relationship with him—did I ever!—but I didn't want one that I had wished into being. I didn't know how to handle that situation, and so I did what I always did when I didn't know what to do: I avoided it. I hadn't returned Alder's calls or texts.

Thyme and I arrived at the store at the same time. "Have you seen Fred since yesterday?" Thyme asked me as I unlocked the door.

"No," I said.

Thyme walked in first. "Perhaps he *has* gone for good, then."

"No." I shook my head. "No, I can feel him around."

Thyme shot me a speculative look. "We have some time before opening. Why don't we see if your baking has improved?"

I stopped at the door to the back room and looked at her. "What do you mean? I don't see a connection."

Thyme gave me a gentle shove. "Get in there and rustle up some plain cupcakes, nothing too fancy, mind you. Remember how we told you that your powers as a witch were tied up with your baking?"

I nodded. "Yes, I remember it well. You told me over hundred times," I added sarcastically.

Thyme was unperturbed. "Did you understand it?"

I sighed. "Yes. Well, no. I have a natural affinity with fire magic because I'm a powerful witch, that why I set cakes on fire when I'm baking."

"That's right."

I shrugged. I had never understood it, and it sure wasn't any clearer to me now.

"And that's why I'm sure your baking has improved."

"What?" I was exasperated.

Thyme's response was to gather flour, eggs, milk, sugar, and butter and deposit them on the countertop. "Amelia Spelled, you make a batch of cupcakes right now!" She put her hands on her hips. "You've started to control your magic, and that goes hand in hand with your baking. Wait and see."

It seemed I had no choice. Thyme handed me the recipe and I prepared to follow it religiously, just as I always did. However, my usual attempts ended in visits from the firefighters as well as insurance claims. My premiums were quite high by now.

After I preheated the oven, I mixed the ingredients. By the time I placed the cupcakes in the oven, Thyme was beaming. I didn't share her enthusiasm. "Only twelve minutes to go!" she announced happily. "You'll see!"

I filled a bucket of water, just to be on the safe side, and then sat next to her. Five minutes later, I was beginning to be little excited. My baking attempts had usually caught on fire by now. Could Thyme have been right?

Finally, the time was up, and there was no smoke in sight. Thyme and I stood up and high fived each other. "Well then, get them out of the oven," she said. "I'll get the cooling rack."

I wasn't quite game. Still, I bravely reached for the oven mitts and gingerly edged toward the oven. I opened the door carefully, expecting a rush of smoke, but there was nothing. With Thyme cheering behind me, I reached in and took out the tray. The tray was awfully heavily, but the cakes were not charcoal, so that was a huge improvement.

Thyme could not get the grin off her face as I tipped the cakes onto the cooling rack. It promptly collapsed, squashed flat. I reached for one of the cakes, but dropped it on the ground. "Yay!" Thyme yelled. "It didn't crack the concrete! The last cake you made that didn't spontaneously combust made a big crack in the concrete!"

I allowed myself to be pleased. This *was* a significant improvement. Perhaps Thyme was right, after all. I tried to stick a knife in the cake, but of course it couldn't penetrate it. I tried another cake, and managed to cut a crust off the edge. "Wow, I really *have* improved," I said with delight. Still, I had no time to rest on my laurels as I had to open the shop.

No sooner had I opened the door than Ruprecht walked in, followed by Camino and Mint. Thyme hurried out to tell them the good news. "You won't believe it! Amelia just baked a small batch of cupcakes, and there wasn't a fire, not even any smoke! And they didn't come out all black."

Ruprecht placed his hand on my shoulder. "I knew you could do it, Amelia. Thyme already told me how you disposed of Fred yesterday. This is all tied in with your baking."

"So Thyme keeps telling me," I said dryly.

"Magic isn't complicated," Ruprecht said with a faraway look in his eyes, "or at least, it doesn't have to be. The practitioner simply needs focus, belief in her or his abilities, and intention. Intention is everything. As Horace said, 'Aequam memento rebus in arduis servare mentem.'"

"Excuse me?" I said. I suspected I had a migraine coming on.

"You know, Horace the famous Roman poet," Thyme said.

I sighed. "I know who Horace is, but I can't understand Latin."

"When life's path is steep, remember to keep your mind even."

My jaw dropped. "Thyme, I didn't know you could speak Latin!"

Everyone, with the exception of Ruprecht, burst into laughter. He was still speaking Latin softy, although this time to himself. "It's one of Grandfather's favorite sayings," Mint said. "The rest of us can't speak Latin. We've just heard the saying along with its translation a million times." She tapped Ruprecht on the arm. "Grandfather, are you going to tell Amelia about Laurence Burleigh?"

"Oh yes, forgive me. Yesterday, I discovered that Scott was blackmailing Laurence."

"You're kidding!" I cast an anxious glance at the door, hoping customers wouldn't come in before I had the chance to hear all about it. "Over what?"

"We don't really have all the details yet, but I suspect that Laurence caught onto Scott's illegal activities, and was about to expose him when Scott found something to implicate Laurence himself."

"Do you know what Laurence did?" I asked him.

Ruprecht nodded. "Yes, but keep this to yourself," he said in a conspiratorial tone. He and his wife pretended they were Catholic so their daughter could go to the Immaculate Conception Ladies College in North Sydney."

"That's it?" I said in disbelief. "Why would anyone care about that?"

Camino patted my arm. "You don't have children yet, dear. That school is all but impossible to get into, and their daughter is there under a scholarship. She'd lose her scholarship as well as her place in the school if anyone found out that her parents weren't Catholic."

"Oh." I couldn't think of a suitable reply. "How did Scott find out that Laurence wasn't Catholic?"

"I have no idea," Ruprecht said. "And I'm sure you're wondering how I found this out."

I nodded.

"Laurence's wife, Betty, is a long-term customer of mine. I called her yesterday and invited her to *Glinda's* to see my new antique Chinese open-carved armoire. When I say 'new,' I mean new to my store, of course, as it was made in 1850 or thereabouts."

Mint interrupted him. "Please tell Amelia what Betty said."

Ruprecht nodded. "Ah yes. I brought the conversation around to the matter of Scott Plank, and she confided in me that he had been blackmailing the

Burleighs for a year, and for a considerable monthly sum at that."

"For enough money to give him a motive for murder?" I asked.

Ruprecht clasped his hands. "What are the usual motives for murder? Love, money, revenge, being in the wrong place at the wrong time." He rubbed his chin thoughtfully. "Whether or not someone murders someone over money depends on the person's own character. Most things, wars for example, prove to be driven by economics. Take Helen of Troy for example. While legend has it that the Trojan War was fought over the famous beauty, the facts are that Troy sat on an important trade route. Economics! There you have it."

"Err, yes," I said, looking at Mint for help.

"Grandfather, how do we follow up this lead on Laurence?" Mint asked him.

"By going straight to the source," Ruprecht replied with a twinkle in his eyes. "I've invited Betty Burleigh for dinner tonight. And I'm inviting all of you as well."

Chapter 21

We were sitting around Ruprecht's ancient oak table. I was watching the candlelight play along the grain. Ruprecht had sprinkled powdered calamus and powdered licorice root under the chair in which Betty would be sitting. The five of us had just finished doing a spell to compel Betty to tell us the truth about anything that would lead us to the discovery of Scott's murderer. Ruprecht looked at his watch. "Everything's organized now. Betty should be here any minute."

Right on cue, the doorbell rang, and Ruprecht presently returned with a short, cheerful woman. "This is Betty Burleigh," he said, and then introduced each of us in turn.

I had set the table while the others had done the cooking. Sure, my baking had improved, but not to the extent of the food being edible. I smiled when the meal was placed in front of us, savoring the aroma of garlic and parmesan cheese. It was infinitely better than my usual frozen microwave fare. "Tagliatelle Bolognese," Camino announced.

Ruprecht produced a bottle of red wine with a flourish. "*Barbera* anyone? It's locally grown, in Mudgee."

"A fine Italian wine," Betty said, "and grown in Australia. Ruprecht, your taste in wine is surpassed only by your taste in antiques."

Ruprecht gave a little bow before pouring everyone a glass. "It has a tart acidity and a cheerful cherry flavor."

For a while, I zoned out as the conversation was all about antiques. "Ruprecht, I'm looking for a bargain oriental rug. There are so many imitations around these days," Betty said sadly.

Ruprecht shook his head. "I don't deal in fabrics at all, but I could give you the names of some contacts."

"I'd like to buy an antique onesie," Camino said to no one in particular. She was staring at her fork as she spoke.

I was startled. "I think they're a modern invention, Camino."

Camino set down her fork and smiled at me. "To the contrary, my dear, onesies were around in the eighteenth century, and then made a comeback in the 1930's."

"Well, you learn something new every day," Thyme said with a chuckle.

The main course had come to an end, and the subject had not yet turned to the matter of Scott Plank. I was a little anxious, but had confidence that Ruprecht knew what he was doing.

Camino and Thyme left the table to fetch dessert. "It's pavlova," Ruprecht announced. "More wine, Betty?"

Betty giggled. "I think I'm already somewhat over-refreshed." Nevertheless, she held out her glass for more.

When everyone was eating pavlova, Ruprecht spoke up. "Betty, we've heard that Scott Plank was a most unscrupulous man, an unsavory character." Betty nodded. "I heard he cheated Kayleen over the sale of some land," Ruprecht added.

Betty sipped her wine before answering. "That's true. He sold her twenty acres out on the Recoil Road. Everybody knows that land's worthless, but he convinced Kayleen to pay a tidy sum. He said it was a secret that the Council was about to put in a sewer pump station. She thought she was onto a good thing. Trouble is, Scott was lying. He said as much to my husband."

"Why would he admit such a thing to your husband?" Thyme asked.

"Scott and Laurence used to be good friends," Betty said. "They exchanged confidences. That was, until Scott must have thought he'd admitted too much to Laurence, and turned against him."

Aha, I thought. *That's how Scott knew that Betty and Laurence weren't really Catholic.*

Betty was still speaking. "Oh course, Laurence didn't approve of Scott's dealings, not at all! He'd often come home from the pub awfully upset, after what Scott had confided in him."

"Do you know who killed Scott?" Ruprecht asked bluntly, but Betty did not appear to take offense.

She shook her head. "It could have been any number of people. Scott wasn't a nice man."

I bit my lip. Betty was under the influence of a truth spell, so if her husband had killed Scott, and Betty had known, she would have told us. And by the way she spoke of their relationship, it didn't seem to me that he'd keep such a thing from her. I really hoped that Fred wasn't the culprit.

"Do you think Kayleen killed him?" I asked hopefully.

"I don't think so. It's possible, I suppose." Betty looked thoughtful. "I also suspect Helen and Henry Harden might've had something to do with it. Goodness knows they had reason."

Everyone around the table sat up straight at that pronouncement.

"Helen and Henry Harden?" Ruprecht said. "Please, go on."

"Scott sold a large parcel land to Helen and Henry Harden for fifteen million dollars. Scott told them that the Council was about to change the zoning to allow it to be subdivided, and that they'd make millions on the deal, but he lied."

"Fifteen million dollars!" Mint exclaimed. "Where would the Hardens get that kind of money?"

Betty looked surprised. "Didn't you know? Helen's father was very wealthy. He died not too long ago, and she was the only beneficiary. Scott moved in for the kill, so to speak. The probate was only just through when Scott sold them the land. They lost everything. They were devastated."

"Do the police know this?" I asked her. "Surely Henry and Helen would be the prime suspects if they knew."

"Laurence told the detectives," Betty said, "but there was no evidence. The police didn't find out anything, because the land was sold from an offshore account. The police would have no way to dig into it and get the facts. The Hardens lost millions of dollars."

"But surely the Hardens' lawyer told them that the property couldn't be subdivided," I said. "Those things are always worked out prior to sale."

Betty pulled a face. "Both parties used the same lawyer, and Scott told Laurence that he'd paid the lawyer a huge cut to do a cover up. That lawyer's now living permanently in Belize, a country that has no extradition treaty with Australia. Anyway, the lawyer changed his name."

"Is it actually legal to have the same lawyer acting for the buyer and seller?" I wondered aloud.

Ruprecht nodded. "Yes. It's perfectly legal in New South Wales if both parties are agreeable."

"And the police couldn't do anything?" I asked Betty.

Betty shook her head. "No. They told Laurence they'd need the numbers of the offshore account, otherwise it was like looking for a needle in a haystack."

Betty left soon after. Ruprecht showed her to the door, and the moment he was back in the room, we all erupted into discussion. Thyme was the first to speak. "Are we all thinking it was the Hardens?"

Mint and I nodded, but Camino dissented. "It still could be Kayleen. The awful woman always cards me, even when she sees I'm home. She's too lazy to deliver packages to me."

Ruprecht took his seat. "I'm inclined to agree with Camino."

"You are?" I hadn't meant it to come out so forcefully.

Ruprecht nodded. "Not about Kayleen as such, but we now know that the Hardens had significant motive to murder Scott. That doesn't necessary mean they are the perpetrators, although it is starting to look likely."

I sighed long and hard. "You're not still thinking it could've been Fred?"

"Fred, Kayleen and Craig, or the Hardens," Ruprecht said. "I'm inclined to believe it wasn't Laurence. That's the one suspect I feel we can exclude. However, my focus is now on the Hardens."

"Great!" I put my head in my hands. I was upset that there was still a possibility that Fred had murdered a man, and I was the one who had summoned him. "You know, this has just occurred to me. I was at Helen Harden's having my back treatment just before Scott was murdered. She seemed cool and collected, normal, if you know what I mean. If she knew her husband was about to murder someone, wouldn't she be acting weird?"

"Perhaps she didn't know," Thyme offered. "We know she wasn't the one who actually did the deed. Perhaps her husband, Henry, murdered Scott and kept it from her."

"And the police are ignoring one valuable piece of evidence," Ruprecht added, "because they would need to know the numbers of Scott's offshore account and evidence that it's linked to him. All we need to do is find that out, and then go the police. That will give them evidence for Henry Harden's motive."

Camino yawned and stretched. "How do we find evidence of Scott's offshore account? His lawyer's now living in Bolivia…"

Mint corrected her. "Belize."

"Oh sorry, Belize." Camino nodded. "I'm sure his lawyer wasn't silly enough to leave a paper trail."

"But surely Henry kept records of his transaction with Scott," Thyme said. "We need to find the numbers of the offshore account. Then it will be up to the police to investigate, but at least we can give them a helping hand."

"Why can't the police find the numbers?" I asked.

"Because they would need a search warrant and they don't have any evidence to get one," Thyme explained with a sigh. "We need those numbers."

"But how?" I said, worried that it was somehow going to involve me. I was right.

"Amelia and I will break into the Hardens' house…" Thyme began.

I cut her off. "Break in? As in break and enter? As in criminal offense with prison time? I don't think so." I shook my head furiously.

Thyme shrugged. "I've thought it all through. Mint can mind the store." She looked at Mint, who nodded. "There's a Council meeting tomorrow morning for all staff, so Henry Harden will have to be there. Amelia, you and I will look through the Hardens' paperwork, computer, whatever. We'll be quite safe, because Camino will book an appointment with Helen Harden, and Ruprecht will go to the Council meeting. Either will call us if one of the Hardens looks like they're leaving. That will make it safe."

Camino looked as unenthusiastic as I was. "What if I can't get an appointment for tomorrow morning?'

"Just wait outside, and call us if she leaves."

"Evil always turns up in this world through some genius or other," Ruprecht said flatly. I knew him well enough by now to recognize the tone as one he used for quoting famous philosophers. I had no idea which philosopher this was, and I hoped he wouldn't tell me. He pressed on. "I'm worried about this scheme of yours, Thyme. It seems to me that it could put both you and Amelia in danger."

"Seriously, I think it will be fine," Thyme said in her most pleading tone. "What can go wrong? The Hardens don't have any kids, and you and Camino can make sure they're both away from their home."

"What if they have security?" Mint asked her. "Back to base alarms, that sort of thing?"

Thyme smirked. "There's a scheduled electrical outage in their area all morning tomorrow.

I know because I live near them. They won't have any power. And Amelia, you said Helen told you they don't have battery backup."

"You really have thought this through, Thyme," Ruprecht said with undisguised admiration.

I held up my hand. "I'm not doing it! It's a crazy idea—no offense, Thyme. I won't do it! I just won't!"

Chapter 22

Thyme and I crouched in a thick wattle bush, a prickly bush at that. We were both wearing black, which Thyme said would make us less noticeable, but I thought made us look like bank robbers with poor taste in clothes.

The Hardens' house was at the end of a long lane. It was an unremarkable house, broad blue weatherboards above a deep red brick base, and could have been pretty with a little care and attention—and a lot of paint. As it was, it appeared to be entirely neglected. Withering jasmine had constricted the down pipes. Yellowed lace curtains hung from dreary windows. The only sound was from native birds and two curious sheep that peered at us through the wire fence.

Thyme handed me a pair of gloves. "Put these on."

I did as she asked. I was still puffing from cutting cross-country. "What do we do now?" I whispered to Thyme.

"We make sure no one is watching us," she whispered back.

Given that the Hardens' house was down the end of a lane, so I couldn't see who could be looking at us, apart from some wood ducks, birds, and the two sheep. I pointed this out to Thyme, and she agreed that we could proceed. Just as we moved off, a kookaburra in the eucalyptus tree above us laughed raucously.

We hurried around the side of the house, and found an open window. This was no surprise, given that people in the country as a rule did not lock their houses, not in by Bayberry Creek anyway.

Suddenly, a man appeared in front of me. I screamed. Thyme clamped her hand over my mouth.

"Great Dark Witch, how may I assist you?"

"Please go away!" I said when Thyme removed her hand.

"Have I done something to offend you, Great One?"

"Aren't you supposed to do what I say?" I said. "Go away, right now."

Fred vanished. Thyme patted my back. "You got rid of him easily that time."

"I just have to figure out how to get rid of him for good," I said. "Can you give me a boost? I think I could fit through that window."

Thyme looked doubtful. "Don't you think I should do it?"

I frowned. "Why?"

She shrugged and then pushed me hard through the small opening in the sash window. "Amelia, have you put on weight?"

"No!" I lied, thinking of my back cleavage. "I've gained muscles, not fat."

Thyme sniggered and then tried to disguise it with a cough.

With one more shove from Thyme, I landed hard on the floor. "Ouch! That hurt!"

"Quick, let me in through the back door!" Thyme whispered.

I picked myself off the shag pile carpet, a particularly hideous shade of burned orange that looked as though it needed a thorough clean, and hurried to the back door. I was thankful I didn't encounter any dogs. I had some treats in my pocket just in case, but so far it didn't seem as if I'd need to use them.

"This house is so 70's," I said, looking at the orange countertops and the patterned tiles.

"We're not here to look for evidence of decorating crimes," Thyme said smugly as she walked into the kitchen.

"I don't want to be here at all," I reminded her.

"You'll thank me when we find evidence that it was Henry and not Fred who killed Scott."

I nodded, wiping my hands on my jeans. I was in a cold sweat, and my heart was beating out of my chest. "Can you check your phone again, Thyme?"

She sighed. "It's still on, just like it was the last time you asked me a minute ago."

I pulled a face. "I don't fancy going to prison."

"Well then, let's get out of here as fast as we can. Do you have your USB on you?"

I pulled it out of my pocket and waved it at her. "I don't know what good it'll do. I don't know his passwords, and I'm not a hacker."

Thyme ignored my remark. "That looks like an office through that door. How about you go in there, and I'll take the bedroom and the rest of the house?"

I hurried into the office. It was a depressing room, musty and dimly lit. The only light was provided by a small sash window over which were draped the most hideous curtains I had ever seen -- paisley patterned in shades of mustard. I pulled open the desk drawer, which thankfully wasn't locked, and looked through the papers. They were mostly electricity and phone bills, along with some tax papers.

There was a large iMac sitting on the edge of the messy desk, so I wondered if all the information was on that. Having the power off wasn't such a benefit, after all. A laptop was sitting next to it. I opened it, and to my surprise, all the windows opened. I couldn't believe my luck. It must have been left on. What's more, the power icon showed it still had an hour of battery remaining. I inserted the USB and then looked for information.

I found Henry's email and clicked on it, and thankfully his user name and password autopopulated. He had dozens of email folders that did not appear to be labeled accurately. I didn't want to waste time scrolling through those, so I opened his documents.

There it was! It was all laid out perfectly: the minutiae of how much and when he had paid Scott—I winced when I saw the figure—and the numbers of the account in Belize.

My hands shook with excitement. I copied it onto the USB as fast as I could. I seized the USB, shut the laptop, and hurried out of the room to find Thyme.

As I rounded the door, she bumped into me. "Quick! Ruprecht just texted. Henry's leaving!"

"Is he coming here?"

Thyme shrugged. "How would Ruprecht know? Ok, we have to get out of here, fast!"

We hurried to the back door. She flicked the latch over and then pulled the door shut behind us. Once safely outside, we peered around the corner of the house. "Can you hear a car?" I asked Thyme.

Thyme shook her head. "No, can you?"

"No. Let's go!"

We sprinted for the cover of the bushes. When we reached the growth of wattle trees, Thyme pulled me down beside her. "We can see the road from here. I can't see anyone coming yet."

"Let's cut across that paddock near the creek."

We sprinted away again, and then ran down a ditch which would hide us from the road. I stopped to draw breath, but Thyme urged me on. We came to the creek crossing. "I can't go over there without getting my shoes wet," Thyme complained, "but we can't risk going the long way."

"This is all your idea," I grumbled, stepping into the fast flowing water. Thankfully, at this point the creek was only a few feet across, but it rose to my knees. I emerged on the other side with squelching shoes and soaked jeans bottoms.

"Oh, I forgot to ask you," Thyme said as she sloshed through the creek. "Did you get anything? I didn't. Just a lot of bills and receipts and a whole lot of boring stuff."

I slapped my forehead. "I forgot got to tell you, since I was so busy running away from the scene of the crime. I got all the information."

"What? You did?"

I nodded. "Yes, it's on the USB."

Thyme hugged me so tightly I was worried she would crush the evidence.

Chapter 23

The plan was that I would go home and have a shower, and Thyme would do likewise, only she would summon Ruprecht to my place. We would all look at the evidence and then decide how to deliver it to the police. I thought the only way was to mail it anonymously, but figured Ruprecht might come up with something better.

I stepped out of the shower to be met by Willow and Hawthorn. It was obvious they both expected to be fed. "It's only midday," I informed them. "I fed you this morning and I'm not feeding you again until tonight."

The cats' eyes widened; their tails swished, and they looked more than displeased. I sighed and went to the kitchen to fetch their bowls. "Just a small snack," I said in defeat.

I went back into my bedroom and took the USB from my dresser. Sitting on my bed, I opened my laptop and copied the file across. I opened the file to check it, and breathed a big sigh of relief that it hadn't somehow been corrupted. Now I had a back up. Just then, the house turned up the TV, so I hurried into the living room to turn it down. I averted my eyes as someone's head was lopped off.

"Please don't turn it up again for a while," I said. "I've had a really hard morning. I'll leave it on, but just not too loud, okay?"

Apparently the house agreed, as the volume remained low.

I hurried around the room, quickly tidying up before Ruprecht and Thyme came. Where did all that cat hair come from? It wasn't as if they were Persians, yet there were dust bunnies, or rather cat hair bunnies, all over the room. I had just disposed of the last of the cat hair when there was a knock on the door. Bummer, I wouldn't have time to vacuum.

I opened the door to see a man standing there. "Great One, it is me, Fred."

"Since when have you ever used doors?" I asked him.

Fred bowed deeply. "Great Dark Witch, I seem to incur your displeasure when I arrive unannounced. Would you be so kind as to allow me to enter your premises?"

I stood back, and he walked inside. I showed him into the living room. I have no idea why I did, but I didn't know what else to do. "I need to ask you a question."

He bowed deeply again.

"Did you murder Scott Plank?"

The spirit took a step backward and clutched his throat. "How could you ask me such a thing,

Great One? I am mortally offended. What must you think of me? No, of course I did not kill anyone!"

"I command you to tell me the truth. I wish you would tell me the truth," I added to cover all my bases.

"Of course I'm telling you the truth, Great One!" His face fell.

I allowed myself to feel some small measure of relief. Of course, I didn't know whether or not he really was telling the truth, but I felt that he was. "You'll have to go now, Fred. Go back to wherever it is that you came from."

Fred appeared to be on the point of crying. "I want to go. I don't like it on this plane of existence. It's boring and drab."

That had never occurred to me. "Why don't you just go?"

Fred looked exasperated. "Because you summoned me, Great One. You're the only one who can send me back."

I at once was contrite. "Oh my gosh, I'm so sorry. I didn't realize."

He narrowed his eyes into tiny slits. "You humans are so parochial, if you'll forgive me for saying so."

"I don't suppose you have any idea how I can send you back?" I asked hopefully.

Fred looked shocked. "You ask *me*, Great One?"

"Okay, okay. I'll do it." I had no idea how I would, but I had to try.

I quieted my mind, and visualized my feet sinking into the ground below me, as I often did with a grounding meditation. First I felt nothing, but that immediately progressed to feeling incredibly strange. There was a ringing in my ears and a metallic taste in my mouth. A distant sound of rushing unnerved me. I focused on my visualization, and then opened myself up to my own nascent power.

There—I had done it. There was no flash of lightning, no crack of thunder. The cloister bells didn't ring. I didn't feel any surges of energy. I was Amelia Spelled, Dark Witch. I had finally come into my power. Yet I didn't feel commanding as such—I felt balanced, in the flow. There was no way to describe it, other than to say I felt grounded.

Fred had gone. I knew before I even opened my eyes. Yet I was not alone.

I turned with a start, and at the same time, the house turned up the volume on the TV. Every muscle in my body froze.

Henry Harden was standing there, his face partially shadowed by the drawn curtains. Every angle of his face exuded menace. His bloodshot eyes were juxtaposed against his pallid complexion.

My first thought was that he had come to kill me. My second thought was that the house must have something planned, given that it had allowed him inside.

"How did you know?' he asked, taking a step toward me.

"That you killed Scott Plank because he swindled you? Was Helen in it with you?"

Henry took another step. "She knows nothing about it. I want the USB."

I gasped. "How did you know?"

"Nanny cam."

"But, but you don't have any kids," I stuttered.

Henry grunted. "We thought the cleaner was stealing money, so I installed a nanny cam disguised to look like a smoke detector. That's how I saw you open my computer. The motion sensor alerted me and streamed the video to my phone. I want the USB. I also want to know who else knows, or were you acting alone?"

"Why did you kill him in my shop?" I asked him.

"It wasn't planned," he said angrily. "I was on my way to buy cupcakes, and I saw Kayleen and Craig leaving your store. They didn't see me, and when I went in, I saw Scott alone so I dispatched him quickly. I'd been carrying that rope around for days, just waiting for my opportunity, so I took it then and there. I thought the cops would blame Craig and Kayleen. That woman reads my mail."

His manner had turned deadly calm. Suddenly, the TV blared. "Turn that down, will you?" He was angry now.

"It's stuck," I said, hoping the house would make its move soon. I fervently hoped the house didn't want us to act out a scene from *Game of Thrones*, because that involved heads being cut off and other unpleasant things.

Henry loomed over me. "Just get me the USB, and then we'll talk," he yelled over the TV volume.

Then you'll kill me, I thought. Before I could do or say anything, he lunged at the TV in what I assume was an attempt to turn down the volume.

Right then, a blue-white mist seeped from the TV screen just as the sound went off. I staggered backward, terrified, even though I knew it was the house doing something.

Henry, however, did not have the benefit of that knowledge. The mist, forming into the figure of a woman, moved toward him, all pale blue and dead and terrifying, its hands outstretched.

He screamed, and then screamed again.

I put my hands over my eyes, and dared to peep through them just as Sergeant Tinsdell and

Constable Dawson burst into the room. Henry flung himself at Tinsdell. "Save me! Save me! It's a White Walker. Don't let it touch me!" He flung himself to the floor and shook violently.

"*Game of Thrones* was on the TV when he arrived," I said. "His um, episode started after that."

"What was he doing here?" Tinsdell asked me.

"He said he killed Scott Plank. He said Scott cheated him out of millions of dollars, and he said he had all the proof on his laptop. He seemed to think I knew this somehow, so he was coming to kill me."

Tinsdell turned to bend over Henry. "Is that right, Mr. Harden?"

"Yes, yes! I'll confess everything. Just don't let it touch me!" He pointed to the place where the ghost had been, but I couldn't see anything now. I didn't know if Henry still could. "Yes, I killed Scott Plank because he cheated me out of money. Millions of dollars! My wife inherited it, and Scott stole it." He tried to say more but it came out as gibberish.

Constable Dawson handcuffed him and pulled him his feet. "But that White Walker didn't have blue eyes," Henry yelled as he was taken away.

Tinsdell stayed in the room with me as Dawson took Henry out. "Are you harmed at all, Miss Spelled?"

I shook my head. "No, he just came here thinking I knew all the information about him and confessed to murdering Scott Plank. Then he saw that *Game of Thrones* was on TV, and the next thing I knew, he was yelling that a White Walker was coming for him. A White Walker is from *Game of Thrones*. On the show they have huge blank blue eyes, hence his reference."

"Yes, thank you for the *Game of Thrones* explanation," Tinsdell said sarcastically. "I myself watch the show, so I know what a White Walker is. What I don't understand is that this is the second unbalanced murderer I've found in your house. What are the chances?"

"Cats," I said simply, and pointed to Willow and Hawthorn who were sitting on the rug. "Just before Henry came, I spent ages picking up their hair. Henry must be allergic to cats, too." I plastered an innocent look on my face.

"It could be black mold, you know," Tinsdell said quite seriously. "Miss Spelled, you should get this house checked out. Black mold is toxic, and it can cause all sorts of symptoms." He stroked his chin. "I don't know if it can send people mad, though."

Before I could respond, Ruprecht, Camino, and Thyme hurried into the room. "Thank goodness you're all right," Ruprecht said.

Camino took off her toad head and adjusted her onesie. "I saw Henry going into your house, so I called the police."

Tinsdell looked at Camino for a while, and then patted me on the shoulder. "Mold, Miss Spelled, mold. *Please* have it checked out."

Chapter 24

I couldn't wait for Sergeant Tinsdell to leave so I could tell the others what had happened. It seems they were just as keen as I was to discuss the news. As soon as Tinsdell had reached the front gate, they all turned to me and plied me with questions. "I hope you don't mind, but after Camino called the police, she called me, and I called Mint," Thyme said. "Mint's on her way here, so that means the shop is shut."

"No, that's fine," I said.

"How did Henry know that we broke into his house?" Thyme asked me.

"He had a nanny cam disguised as a smoke alarm. It streamed the image to his phone. He saw me at his computer and realized what I was up to."

"But they don't have any kids," Thyme said.

"He thought the cleaner was stealing his money," I explained to her. "Anyway, he came here to try to get the USB back and obviously to kill me, I suppose." I shivered as I said it. "Oh, and how could I forget! A ghost came out of the TV."

"A ghost?" Ruprecht said after a pause.

"Yes, a ghost that looked like a woman came out of the TV. That's what made Henry lose the plot. The house was watching *Game of Thrones* at the time, and he was screaming that a White Walker came out of the TV at him."

Thyme and Camino laughed, but Ruprecht looked solemn. "Is that what he told the police?" Ruprecht asked.

I nodded.

"We will have to stop murderers coming into your house," Ruprecht said seriously, "because that's two now that the house has driven mad. That won't look good to the police."

I frowned at him. Had he realized what he had just said? I rubbed my temples. I was saved from further comment by a knock at the door. "That must be Mint now."

I went to the door and opened it, but there was Alder, with Mint standing behind him. Both looked decidedly awkward. I held the door open. "Come inside, both of you." I showed them into the living room which was only a few steps away. No one looked pleased to see Alder.

They all muttered polite greetings to each other, and then Alder took me by the arm. "Amelia, could I have a word with you?"

I nodded. "Sure. Come into the kitchen."

Alder wasted no time in coming to the point. "I saw the police heading to your place, so I followed them. It was all I could do to wait outside and not race in to see if you were all right." He put his hands on my shoulders and pulled me to him. "Are you okay? You weren't hurt?"

My heart raced at his proximity, but I hurried to assure him that I was fine. "There's something I have to know. By the way, I sent Fred back to where he came from." Alder looked impressed. I tried to find the words, because what I had to say would be embarrassing. In the end, I just blurted it out. "I wondered if Fred had made you kiss me, in your apartment?"

I had never seen Alder look so surprised. "You're serious?"

My cheeks burned. "Yes. He was like an old fashioned genie. You know, if I said aloud that I wished something, he would make it happen."

Alder took a step closer to me. "You said aloud that you wished I'd kiss you?"

I looked at the ground. "Err, yes, in your bathroom. I thought Fred had heard me and then made you kiss me. That he'd somehow magically influenced you to kiss me."

There was silence, so I looked up. Alder appeared to be amused. "Haints can't get into my apartment."

"They can't? Why not?"

"Well, for a start, my porch ceilings are painted haint blue. Apart from that, my house is heavily warded. I also use red brick dust, eggshells, sigils, and other measures I won't mention aloud, but I'm happy to show you."

I was beyond happy. Alder had kissed me because he wanted to kiss me, not because he was Fred-induced. I was on cloud nine.

"So you thought I kissed you because the haint made me?"

I nodded, embarrassed. I was going to say something, but I didn't have the opportunity.

Alder pulled me to him and kissed me thoroughly.

I heard a noise in the hallway so I made to pull away, but he kept his arms around me. I felt his large hands on the small of my back, the warmth of them pulsating through my thin cotton shirt. I shivered with pleasure, my stomach doing somersaults. His breath felt hot and damp against my cheek, and, upon glancing up, I noticed for the first time the length of his eyelashes. *Men shouldn't have such beautiful long eyelashes*, I thought. *It's hardly fair*.

"What are you thinking about?" he asked me, a smile spreading across his face.

I grinned. "Well," I replied, but then my thoughts trailed off. This had been more than just a kiss, had it not? This had been the start of our future together. "Nothing. It's silly. What are you thinking?"

"That this could be the start of our future together."

Oh gosh, he can't read my mind, can he? I thought. Aloud I said, "You're quite the romantic."

He smiled again. "Oh, so you weren't thinking the same?"

"There's a reason people say, 'A penny for your thoughts.' I'm not telling you my thoughts for free."

"People don't use pennies anymore in Australia. Haven't since the 1960's."

"Well then," I replied, "you'll have to kiss me again instead."

"Ahem."

I jumped when I saw Thyme standing in the doorway. I wondered how long she'd been there. I would certainly ask her later. To my relief, she wasn't scowling, but seemed amused. Perhaps her opinion of Alder had improved.

Less than an hour later, the six of us were in my living room, five of us eating pizza, while the house was watching *Game of Thrones*, albeit with the volume turned down. Ruprecht and Alder were discussing philosophers in an amicable fashion, although I overheard them say more than once that they were "in scholarly disagreement." Camino was asleep on the couch, snoring loudly, and both cats were sitting on her stomach.

"That explains it all," Ruprecht said to Alder. "It's always nice to have all the loose ends tied up. Now, it's only occurred me to me in hindsight that the haint probably didn't grant wishes in a genie-type of way after all."

"Is that true?" I wondered aloud.

"Truth is a social construct," Alder and Ruprecht said in unison and then looked at each other and smiled.

I breathed a sigh of relief and contentment. The house would soon tire of *Game of Thrones*, and would move onto something else. No doubt Camino would buy another animal onesie, and my baking would continue to improve. Who knows, one day I might even go so far as to bake something edible. Ruprecht and Thyme were now accepting of Alder, and Mint and Camino would come around soon enough. The magnificently magnetic Alder Vervain and I were at the beginning of a relationship. I shivered happily at the little thrill of excitement that ran through me at that thought.

All was well in my world.

Next Book in this Series.

ExSpelled (The Kitchen Witch Book FIVE)
Spurred on by her recent success in the kitchen, Amelia enrolls in cooking school, yet her baking incurs the wrath of the teachers. Soon after, her classmates begin to die one by one. Can she find the killer before she is expelled, or worse still, becomes the next victim?

The Halloween Spell (The Kitchen Witch Book SIX)
An elderly woman arrives on Amelia's doorstep claiming Amelia's departed Aunt Amelia did a spell for her every Halloween. She insists that Amelia do the spell for her, and that's when the trouble starts.

Other books by Morgana Best.

A Ghost of a Chance (Witch Woods Funeral Home Book 1)
Nobody knows that Laurel Bay can see and talk to ghosts. When she inherits a funeral home, she is forced to return from the city to the small town of

Witch Woods to breathe life into the business. It is a grave responsibility, but Laurel is determined that this will be no dead-end job.

There she has to contend with her manipulative and overly religious mother, more than one ghost, and a secretive but handsome accountant.

When the murder of a local woman in the funeral home strangles the finances, can Laurel solve the murder?

Or will this be the death of her business?

Note: This book is humorously irreverent in places, so please read only if you won't be offended.

Christmas Spirit (The Middle-aged Ghost Whisper Book 1)

Prudence Wallflower tours the country, making live appearances. She connects people with loved ones who have passed on. However, her reputation as a psychic medium is failing, and even Prudence has begun to doubt herself. She has never seen a ghost, but receives impressions from the dead. This all changes when the ghost of a detective appears to her and demands her help to solve a murder. Prudence finds herself out of her depth, and to make matters worse, she is more attracted to this ghost than any man she has ever met.

Series by Morgana Best.
The Kitchen Witch
1) Miss Spelled
2) Dizzy Spells
3) Sit for a Spell
4) Spelling Mistake
5) Ex-Spelled
6) The Halloween Spell

The Middle-aged Ghost Whisperer
1) Christmas Spirit
2) Ghost Hunter

Witch Woods Funeral Home
1) A Ghost of a Chance
2) Nothing to Ghost About
3) Make the Ghost of It

And Morgana's non-Witch Cozy Mysteries:
Cocoa Narel Chocolate Shop Mysteries
1) Sweet Revenge
2) The Sugar Hit

The Australian Amateur Sleuth
1) Live and Let Diet
2) Natural-Born Grillers
3) Dye Hard

4) The Prawn Identity
5) Any Given Sundae

About Morgana Best.

#1 Best-selling Cozy Mystery author, Morgana Best, lives in a sunny beachside town in Australia. She is owned by one highly demanding, rescued cat, and two less demanding dogs, a chocolate Labrador and a rescued Dingo, as well as two rescued Dorper sheep, the ram, Herbert, and his wether friend, Bertie.

Morgana is a former college professor who now writes full time.

In her spare time, Morgana loves to read cozy mysteries and walk her dogs along the beach.

Made in the USA
Middletown, DE
10 September 2016